THE TROUBLE WITH GOODBYE

Fairhope, Book 1

SARRA CANNON

Dead River Books

CHAPTER 1

My stomach twists as the sign for Harrison's Pecan Farm comes into view.

Exactly twelve miles from the house I grew up in and swore I'd never move back to.

And even though I've driven almost a thousand miles to get here, I'm still not ready for that sign. Not yet.

I turn onto the gravel road, deciding to take the long way instead of going through downtown. It's midnight on a Friday night which means lots of people I used to know are riding around town and hanging out, drinking. Someone is bound to recognize my car and start up the rumor mill. I don't want to risk it. I'm going to need a good night's sleep before I'm ready to be the old Leigh Anne.

With any luck, I won't even have to face my parents tonight. They're usually in bed by ten, so maybe I can sneak in and postpone the questions and the lectures until tomorrow.

The car vibrates as I roll over the loose gravel. Smoky-gray dust rises up around me. Ghosts of my past life come back to haunt me. Ten minutes ago, I could barely keep my eyes open, but now I'm wide awake and wishing I had another hundred miles to go.

From the side of the road, movement draws my eye and I slam on the brakes as a trio of deer runs out in front of my car. I'm going too fast. I turn the steering wheel, remembering my granddaddy's warning to always hit a big animal at an angle instead of straight-on. Only, I realize too late that I've yanked the wheel way too hard.

The tires slip against the small rocks and the car lurches sideways, throwing my shoulder hard against the door as the vehicle skids off the road and into the ditch. My right foot presses hard against the brake pedal, but it's too little, too late. I've managed to miss the deer, but there's no way around that tree. I brace myself for impact and hold my breath.

There's a brief moment where I think, *this is it.*

My whole life doesn't exactly flash before my eyes the way they say it will before you die. No, it's just one night that comes to mind.

And as it does, I almost hope this is the end.

A scream is ripped from my throat as my body jerks forward violently. The windshield shatters into a million pieces that fly into my hair and lap. It all happens so fast. There's less than a full second of the loudest noise I've ever heard as the metal bends and groans, but then everything comes to an abrupt stop.

I sit there, my body tense, my fingers wrapped around the steering wheel in a death-grip, and I force myself to breathe.

My legs tremble and my heart hammers against my ribs.

What. The. Fuck.

I can't move. I can't think. I can only sit and stare and breathe in and out.

Gradually, I manage to pull my shaking hands from the wheel and unbuckle the seat belt that's now cutting off my circulation. Tiny shards of glass fall from my skin and clothes as

I move, but I don't think I'm cut. My shoulder throbs and my neck is sore, but other than that, I'm okay.

My mind is spinning, but I'm coherent enough to know I should call someone. Get help.

I reach for my phone and pause. Who do I call? If my parents come out here and see this mess, they are going to totally freak out. They're already going to be in major over-protective mode right now, so the image of me almost dying in a car accident is going to tempt them to lock me in a closet until I'm twenty-five.

I shake my head and tears spring to my eyes. Who else would I call? I've barely talked to any of my old friends since I left for school two years ago. It's not like I can just call them up in the middle of the night and make small talk until it seems appropriate to mention I've smashed my car into a tree and could really use a ride home.

No, there's no one else. I dial my dad's cell phone and press the phone to my ear. I wait.

Nothing happens. I pull the phone away and stare at it, dazed. What the hell is wrong with this thing?

Then, through the haze of confusion in my brain, I remember I'm not in Boston anymore. I'm literally in the middle of nowhere. I check for bars, but all I see is a sad little 'x' that means I have no service out here in the woods.

Perfect.

I clench my teeth and toss the phone back into the cup holder. Now what? Walk? I'm not even sure I can pull it together enough to stand up, much less walk ten miles. In the dark. In flip-flops.

Maybe I'll have better luck with service out on the road.

I reach for the handle and push against my door. It creaks slightly, then groans and refuses to budge another centimeter. I put more of my weight behind it, but the door won't move.

3

The passenger side is completely fucked. The metal is gnarled and twisted and the seat is completely destroyed. There's no chance I'm going out that way.

I'm stuck unless I can work up the nerve to crawl through the broken windshield.

I sit back against the seat and swallow the lump forming in my throat. After everything else, is this really happening to me? The weight of the world feels like it's coming down on my shoulders. I stare at the pieces of glass and realize that's what I've become.

Broken.

Headlights flash and bounce along the bumpy road behind me. I turn around to get a better look, but my neck screams in pain. I push my head back against the seat and press my lips together in a grimace. My eyes close and the world inside my head spins violently. I think I'm going to throw up.

I hear the car slow and then grind to a halt up on the road. I don't dare turn around again, but relief floods through me just knowing someone is coming to help. I just pray it's someone I know and not some lunatic murderer.

Of course, what are the chances a murderer would really stop to help? I laugh at the thought, but my throat is dry and it makes me cough instead.

A door slams and footsteps rustle through the grass.

"Oh, my god." He says it in a whisper, but it sends chills along my spine. Things must look pretty bad from out there.

"I'm okay," I say in a scratchy voice, turning my head slightly so I can get a look at my rescuer. "It looks a lot worse than it is, but I think the door is stuck."

All I can see in the darkness is a tall, muscled figure. He's wearing a baseball cap, and I can't quite make out his face.

"I'm gonna help get you out of there," he says. "Hold on a sec."

The door groans in protest, but finally gives up and flies open. A warm breeze sails across my bare legs, and I shiver as it begins to sink in that this could have ended much worse. A hand reaches out. I place mine inside and his fingers wrap tight around my own.

"Careful, now. You might be hurt more than you realize," he says. "Just take it real slow and stop if anything hurts."

I take his advice and move with caution, putting one foot on the ground. Then the other. I use his hand to steady myself and pull up, but my legs are weaker that I expect. My knees buckle and my eyes lose focus. Strong arms circle around to catch me and lift me up, away from the car. On instinct, my arms reach around his neck. I lean against his chest and concentrate on the steady beat of his heart and the sound of the tall grass zipping along his jeans.

He turns to the side and manages to open the passenger-side door of his truck. Light spills across the road and country music plays low on the radio.

He sets me gently on the cracked leather seat, then pulls away so I can see his face for the first time. I'm surprised to see he's around my age. There's a couple day's-worth of dark stubble on his face and a streak of something black, like oil or soot, on his right cheek.

But it's his eyes that capture me.

They are the clearest, brightest blue I've ever seen. An electric jolt flashes through me. My arms break out in goose bumps, and I have no idea whether it's from the shock of the accident or the feel of his hand against mine.

He stares at me with concern wrinkling his forehead.

"Are you sure you're okay?" He glances back toward the car. "I didn't know what to expect when I got down there. I thought..."

He doesn't complete his thought, but I know what he means to say.

I blink and shake my head. "I think I'm still a little out of it."

I break my eyes away from his face and really look at myself for the first time in the light. Shards of glass still cling to my tank top, but I don't see a single scratch anywhere on my body. The only pain I feel is the throbbing of my left shoulder. I turn my neck to get a closer look and see if there's a bruise or scrape, but just like before, a terrible pain shoots through me from my neck all the way down my shoulder and back. I cry out and reach up to massage the spot.

"That doesn't sound good," he says.

He leans forward and out of habit, I jerk back. My eyes are wide and a lump forms in my throat. The reaction makes no sense, because I'd just let him carry me all the way up here. Still, there's a part of my subconscious that knows I'm all alone with a stranger and that I'm vulnerable. Even now, after a year and a half, I still carry that fear with me, somewhere deep inside.

I'm immediately embarrassed and try to laugh it off. "Sorry, I'm still a little jumpy I guess."

"It's fine," he says gently, those blue eyes locked on mine. "Is it your shoulder that hurts?"

"I think I slammed it against the door when the car swerved," I say, still rubbing my neck. "And every time I try to turn my neck to the left, it hurts like fuck."

"Whiplash, probably," he says. "I would call 911 or something but I don't have any cell service out here."

"Me either. That was the first thing I checked."

"I'm gonna get you to the hospital."

I shake my head. "No, I just want to go home," I say. Coming back to Fairhope was supposed to be all about simplifying my life and getting away from all the drama. The last thing I want is to spend the night in Fairhope Memorial's shitty emergency room. It would be the talk of the town by noon tomorrow, and by Sunday the story would be something outrageous like how I drove into town drunk, and, going a hundred miles an hour, crashed into a tree.

"You sure? It might be a good idea just to have someone take a look," he says. "Injuries from car accidents can be tricky. You didn't hit your head or anything did you?"

"I'm fine," I say. "Just a little bit sore. I've been driving since yesterday and all I want to do is just go home, get a shower and get into bed. Maybe sleep for a week."

He smiles and even though his lips just barely turn up at the corners, his eyes light up from the inside.

My breath catches in my chest and my cheeks flush with warmth.

It's been a really long time since I reacted to a guy's smile like that, and all I can guess is that the shock of the accident has me all flustered and turned around. I'll probably run into him again next week and realize he's a troll or that he only has mediocre blue eyes. Nothing special.

Of course, it occurs to me now that I don't even know his name or if he lives around here or not.

"I'm Leigh Anne, by the way," I say. "Seriously, thanks for pulling over. I think I would have been stuck in there till morning if it wasn't for you."

"Knox," he says. "Knox Warner."

He holds his hand out to me and for the second time tonight, I take it.

CHAPTER 2

L uckily the damage to my car is confined to the front half, which means most of my clothes and things are fine. Knox empties the trunk in no time, tossing my suitcases and boxes into the back of his truck. I feel a little stupid just sitting here watching from the road while he trudges in and out of the ditch collecting my things, but I'm not sure I would be much help anyway.

Honestly, I'm not sure I could stand up if I wanted to.

I realize I'm clenching my hands together so tight, my knuckles have gone white. I take a deep breath and slowly release the tension in my arms and hands. When I hold them out in front of me, they are still trembling a little.

"Is there anything else you need from inside?" Knox stands next to the bed of the truck, one hand on the rusted metal.

I shake my head. "I don't think so," I say. But I'm wrong. "Oh, no, wait. My cell phone is in the cup holder in the front and my purse is under the seat on the passenger side. I have no idea if you'll even be able to reach it."

Knox nods. "I'll get it," he says. I study him as he runs back down the hill toward my car. There's a quiet confidence to this guy, and I wonder what his story is. He didn't grow up around here or I'd recognize him. He must go to the local university. That's the only thing that really draws people our age to this area.

Well, that and the factory. Of course, last I heard, the factory hasn't been hiring for a while and business is struggling around here.

He disappears inside the car and emerges a few seconds later holding up the phone and my purse triumphantly.

"Got 'em."

I smile. "Thanks."

He comes around the front of the old truck and gets in behind the wheel. He hands over the two items, but there's something else in his hand. He holds it out to me and I open my palm. "I saw this on the floor and thought maybe you'd want it too."

He drops a silver necklace in my hand, and I gasp. My mouth falls open and the tears that threatened to fall earlier are back.

I lift the necklace so I can make sure it really is what I think it is.

A silver pendant dangles from the chain, swinging back and forth. I lay it against the back of my hand and turn the pendant around to see the word etched there.

Believe.

I run a finger across the engraving and a memory flashes through me like it was yesterday. My grandmother sitting on my bed the day before I left for college. She held a Tiffany's box out to me with a sneaky smile on her lips.

"So you'll always remember to believe in yourself," she'd said.

A tear slips down my cheek and I close my fist around the necklace, then wipe away the waterworks.

Knox is staring at me and I look up, expecting to see that look guys get when girls cry. That, *I-have-no-idea-what-to-say-and-I-wish-you'd-just-stop,* look.

Instead, he looks sad. Worried.

I must look worse than I think.

I sniff and stare up at the ceiling, begging the tears to stop. "Sorry," I say with a laugh. "It's just that I thought I'd lost this."

He nods, but doesn't interrupt. He also doesn't ignore me and start driving away. He waits. Listens.

So I keep talking. "My grandmother gave it to me right when I left Fairhope to go off to school," I explain. "She died a few weeks later. It was a total shock to all of us."

"I'm sorry," he says.

"No, don't be." I look up into those blue eyes that have me completely mixed up. "You have no idea how much it means to me that you found this. I thought I'd looked everywhere. I was sick about it when I couldn't find it."

"The wreck must have jostled it loose from wherever it was hiding," he says. "It caught my eye right as I was about to walk away."

My face crumples and I lift the back of my fist to my mouth, trying to hold it all back. I realize he will probably think I'm a lunatic for losing my shit five minutes after we met, but I can't help it. I've been so careful to hide my emotions over the past few weeks, but now, suddenly, grief washes over me. Consumes me.

I lean forward and bury my face in my hands. I turn away as a sob escapes my lips. My body shakes with it and I struggle for air against the crushing weight of guilt and sorrow and anger. Everything I haven't been allowed to feel or express breaks loose, and I don't have the strength to control it anymore.

I don't know what I'm expecting him to do, but so this stranger, this guardian angel, knows exactly what I need.

He scoots across the leather bench seat. Without a word, he pulls me into his arms.

And he lets me cry.

CHAPTER 3

I stare out at the big brick house where I grew up. The front porch light is on, but the window in my parent's bedroom on the second floor is dark. I breathe a sigh of relief. I'm not sure I can handle a fresh lecture about my car. I know they'll be pissed I didn't call the insurance company right away, but it can wait until tomorrow as far as I'm concerned.

I twist the large rusted handle and the door of the truck creaks open.

Knox gets out and goes around to the back to start unloading my things. I join him, taking the smaller suitcase and my large duffel bag.

"If you just set it all here, I can carry it in," I say.

He ignores me and picks up the larger suitcase and one of the big boxes. "I got it," he says. His eyes drift over the neighborhood and he gives a subtle shake of his head before looking at me. "Just lead the way."

There's no use arguing, so I lead him up the walkway toward the front door. It takes three trips for us to get all my stuff onto the porch. I set down the box I'm carrying and reach under the fake potted plant and grab the key.

Before I unlock the door, though, I turn to Knox. I'm not sure how to even say thank you for what he's done for me tonight. I'm still holding the silver chain in my fist and I fidget with it as we stand there.

"I really appreciate everything," I say, but it doesn't sound like enough. He'd held me for almost half an hour before I finally calmed down enough to say a word, which basically means this guy deserves the Olympic Gold Medal for kindness. The fact that he doesn't even know me at all makes it practically evidence for sainthood.

I open my mouth to say something more, but before I get the chance, the door beside me flies open.

My heart drops to my stomach when I see the look on my mother's face. She's already judged this situation and she's already pissed.

"Leigh Anne?" She looks from me to Knox with a very deliberate turn of her head. She lifts her chin and grips the edge of the door. "What on earth is going on here? We were expecting you home hours ago."

"I know, I'm sorry," I say. I spit the story out fast so she doesn't have time to jump to any other conclusions about why I'm standing here in the middle of the night with a strange guy. "A deer ran out in front of my car and I swerved and ended up in a ditch instead. I didn't have any cell service to call you, but luckily Knox here was driving by at just the right time. He was kind enough to load my things in his truck and bring me home."

"Good grief. How many times have I told you to slow down and pay better attention when you're driving at night?" She makes a clicking sound with her tongue. "Is the car okay? It's practically brand new, Leigh Anne."

Knox clears his throat, but doesn't say anything. I look up at him and he raises an eyebrow, probably waiting for me to come clean on just how fucked the car really is. But I'll tell her later. Right now, all I want is to get upstairs and crawl into bed.

"Do you know Knox, Mom?" I change the subject and it seems to distract her for the moment.

She narrows her eyes at him, then leans over to get a better look at the beat-up old truck he's driving. "No, I don't believe I've had the pleasure." She smiles, but her tone is filled with venom disguised as honey. Someone who doesn't know her might not be able to pick up on it, but I recognize it right away. She uses it when she's thinking something nasty about someone but doesn't feel it's socially appropriate to say it out loud. "Are you a student here at the university?"

"No, ma'am," he says, taking me a bit by surprise. "I'm not really the college type."

My mother tugs at her robe, pulling it tighter across her body. "Oh. Well, it's not for everyone, I suppose," she says. An awkward silence falls around us. "Thank you very much for bringing my daughter home safely. You have a good night, now."

She's basically kicking him off her property, and I am infinitely embarrassed by her rudeness.

"Thank you, ma'am." He nods his head toward her, then looks at me. "It was really nice to meet you, Leigh Anne."

"You too," I say. "Hopefully I'll run into you around town sometime."

"I hope so," he says.

He holds my gaze and I get the feeling he wants to say something else. Instead, he turns and nods again to my mother before heading back toward his truck.

I watch him go and feel the pull of regret. We shared something intense and I let him see me more vulnerable than anyone has in a very long time. If ever. It's strange to see him just walk away without there being something more between us. Of

course, between my crazy sobbing and my mother's condescending tone, he's probably more than happy to be getting the
hell out of here.

The truck's engine turns over a couple of times before it
sputters to life. Knox throws it into gear and raises his hand in a
half wave, then drives away, leaving me with a strange hollow
feeling in my stomach.

CHAPTER 4

"Don't just stand there putting on a show for all the neighbors," she says. It's one of her favorite expressions and I swear I'd be a millionaire if I had a dollar for every time I'd heard it growing up. "I'll get your father up and have him bring your things in."

I pick up the overnight bag that has my toothbrush and other toiletries inside. "I hate to wake him up. I can bring them in."

"Don't be silly, I got it," my father calls from half-way down the staircase.

He opens his arms and pulls me into a big bear hug. I lay my head against his chest and catch the faint scent of his aftershave.

"How was your trip, pumpkin?"

"She put her car in a ditch," Mom says. "Some scruffy guy brought her home. Scared me to death. I thought someone was trying to break into the house. I was in the kitchen waiting for you to come through the back door like you always do. Then I looked out and saw that truck. My heart nearly stopped."

I want to scream. She's so judgmental, it makes me want to pull all my hair out. "Well, if he hadn't passed by when he did, I would have been stuck out there for who knows how long," I remind her.

"Thank goodness you're okay," Dad says. "What happened?"

I tell him about the deer.

His face twists with worry. "You were out on Harrison Farm Road? I'm telling you, that road is so dangerous. You're probably the sixth or seventh person to get run off that road by a deer in the past couple years," he says. He moves past me and begins bringing my things in and setting them down on the hardwoods. "I've stopped driving out that way all together if I can help it."

"Guess we're going to have to call Milton and ask him to go out and get the car in the morning," Mom says.

"Any idea where you were on the road?" Dad asks as he brings in the last of the boxes and closes the door. "Or will he be able to see it fine from the road?"

I know I should mention that the car is completely totaled, but I don't have the energy. "Can't miss it," I say.

My mother walks over and hugs my shoulders awkwardly. It's the first time she's attempted to hug me or welcome me home since she opened the door. "I know coming back here isn't exactly what you had planned, but I really think it's for the best," she says. She pats my hand. "Once you get settled, you'll see. You'll finally be able to put this whole thing behind you, once and for all."

I tense and pull away, reaching again for the bags at my feet. "I'm really tired," I say. "It's been a really long couple of days."

"Of course," she says. She reaches up and brushes my hair from my eyes. "Get some sleep. It'll be nice to have you sleeping safe and sound in your own bed tonight."

"Good night," I say. I give each of them a quick kiss on the cheek, then head up the stairs and around the corner to my old room.

Once inside, I throw my bags on the floor and shut the door behind me. I flip on the light and feel the weight of the past press against my shoulders. A past I thought I'd exchanged for some great adventure.

I'm still clutching the necklace in my hand. I walk over to my dresser and lay it across the top, brushing my fingertips across the engraving.

I wish my grandmother was still alive so I could talk to her about all this. I wish I knew the right thing to do. But I stopped believing in myself a long time ago.

Exhaustion weighs me down and I turn toward the bed. I don't even bother brushing my teeth or changing my clothes. I reach up and pull the chain on the ceiling fan, plunging the room into complete darkness. I find my way under the covers and pull them tight around me, finally surrendering myself to sleep.

CHAPTER 5

It's almost noon before I roll out of bed and get in the shower. I turn the water up as hot as it will go and take my time.

When I'm dressed and I know I can't avoid it any longer, I head downstairs to the kitchen where I know I'll find my mother.

"Good morning." There's a knot in my stomach as I wait for her to tear me apart for destroying the car. I'm sure Milton's called by now to say the car was in a lot worse shape than I let on.

Mom sets her coffee mug down on the table and jumps up from her spot. Her arms wrap around my neck and she pulls me close, shocking the hell out of me. This is so not the reaction I was expecting.

I put my arms around her and suddenly we're really hugging each other for the first time in years.

"Oh, Leigh Anne, why didn't you tell us how bad your accident was last night?" Her voice is a scratchy whisper. She pulls out of the hug and takes both of my hands in hers. She looks me up and down. Her forehead is fixed in a worried series of harsh wrinkles. "We should have taken you straight to the emergency room. Milton sent me a snapshot of that car and, oh my god, you could have been killed."

There are actual tears forming in her eyes. I don't know what to say.

"I didn't want you to be mad about the car." As soon as the words hit my tongue, I know I sound like a scared teenager rather than a twenty-year-old woman.

"Your father and I don't care about that car. We can always just buy you a new one," she says. "I feel awful for the way I acted last night. I should have been kissing that boy's feet for rescuing you and bringing you home. I can't imagine how scared you must have been."

I shrug, but I'm actually really relieved. One less argument that needs to happen between us.

"I'm not hurt," I say, not that she's actually asked me how I'm feeling. "My shoulder and my neck are both sore, but it's nothing major."

"Here, come sit down." She pulls a chair out from the table and pats the back of it. "Do you want some coffee? I have some stuff to make sandwiches if you're hungry. Or pancakes? Do you want me to make you some pancakes?"

I smile, then walk past her to get my own mug out of the pantry. "I can get my own coffee, Mom, it's fine."

Her shoulders relax and she nods. "Of course you can," she says. She sits back down at her place where she's been reading a gardening magazine. "Did you want to eat lunch here, then? Or go out? We could go to the club if you wanted to get out of the house for a while. Why don't you give Preston or Penny a call? Let them know you're back in town. They'll be dying to see you."

Preston is the guy I dated for two years in high school. The guy my mother desperately wants me to end up with, even now. Probably especially now.

Penny is his twin sister and was my best friend growing up.

I should want to see them, but the thought of facing them right now makes me feel nauseous. Will they be able to tell I'm different?

I pour my coffee and fill it with cream and sugar. "I think I want to stay kind of close to home for a few days if that's okay," I say. "I'm not sure I'm ready to face everyone right now."

She presses her lips into a thin line. "I know it's been tough for you the past year, but I really think you will be so glad you decided to come home."

We've had this conversation before. She never wanted me to go off to school in the first place, so as soon as she found out what happened, she was pushing me to move back home. At the time, I swore I would never move back here. Not because of him. It would be like giving him some kind of control over me.

When Molly came forward a few months ago, I just couldn't handle it anymore.

"Besides, it's not like any of your friends know what happened, thank goodness." She flips the page of her magazine.

I grip my mug tighter. She is completely clueless about what I'm going through. About what I've been going through all this time. All she thinks about is how it would look if the truth got out. She worries what her friends would think and how prospective rich husbands might pass right on by if they knew I was damaged goods.

She doesn't come out and say all those things, but I know her well enough to know that's what she means.

I want to tell her that no one knowing is part of the problem. It's not easy to carry a secret like this around and never be able to really talk to anyone about what it was like for me. The thought of hanging out with all my friends and having to pretend I'm the same—that this event has not altered me forever—is pure torture. She thinks by moving here and slipping back into my old life, I'll be able to move on and forget.

Only, this isn't the kind of thing I can forget. I've tried.

Instead, it hangs over me like a shroud and with every day that goes by, I feel more and more alone in this world.

I know she doesn't understand. She truly thinks she's doing what's best for me. And I don't know. Maybe she's right. Maybe Fairhope is where I belong.

Where I've always belonged.

I just need a few days to convince myself of that before I dive head-first back into a life I thought I left behind.

CHAPTER 6

The following afternoon, I'm just stepping out of the shower when the doorbell rings.

I throw on a pair of jeans and a pink tank top and poke my head out of my bedroom door, listening. Mom answers the door, and I recognize the voice of the visitor instantly.

Penny.

Excitement and dread clash inside my stomach. I've missed her so much, but at the same time, I'm scared I won't have anything to say to her anymore. Or, that I'll be so different she'll instantly know I'm broken.

"Where is she? I'm dying to see her."

"She's—" My mother begins, but she doesn't need to finish.

As soon as I step onto the top of the stairs, Penny squeals and throws her arms open wide. "Leigh Anne!"

I smile and run down the steps to meet her. We hold tight to each other for a long time and I wonder what I was so nervous for.

"I cannot believe you're actually home," she says when we finally pull apart. "Let me look at you."

She steps back and studies me from head to toe.

"I don't know how it's possible, but I think you've actually gotten more beautiful," she says. "You bitch."

I laugh and run my fingers through my wet hair. "Shut up, my hair is dripping wet and I don't even have any makeup on." I motion for her to follow me up the stairs. My mom waves and retreats to the kitchen. "You're the one who looks amazing. Look at your hair!"

She twirls on the landing and strikes a pose. "You like it?"

"I love it."

Penny has always had very long, dark hair. In fact, she went for years in high school refusing to let a single hair be cut. When I left Fairhope, her hair had been well past her ass. Now, though, it's cut in a stacked bob that's short in the back and gets gradually longer in the front. She also looks like she's lost about twenty pounds.

"I thought you were never going to cut your hair," I say. We get to my bedroom and I grab a brush from my bathroom sink. "When did you change your mind?"

"Gosh, it's been probably a year now," she says. "I change it all the time. It's like once I gave in and decided to change my hair, I got addicted to it. And I've been working out like a crazy person, not that Mason seems to notice."

A wave of guilt washes over me. We used to share absolutely everything and now it's been more than a year since I've even spoken to her. Mason is Preston's best friend and she's had a huge crush on him for forever. I can't believe she's still hung up on him after all this time.

"I really should have kept in touch better," I say.

"I know, me too," she says, hugging me again. "I missed you like crazy. When your mom called mine and said you were home, I almost died. I seriously couldn't get here fast enough. Why didn't you tell me you were coming home for the summer? You should have called me the second you got into town."

I bite my tongue. My mom was always doing this sort of thing. Even though I told her I wanted to take this one step at a time and ease back into life here in Fairhope, she took matters into her own hands. Indirectly, of course, but still incredibly manipulative.

"It was kind of a last minute decision," I tell her. "I needed a couple of days just to recover from the drive." Not exactly the truth, but true enough.

"I'm sure, and Mom said you were in some kind of car accident out near Harrison's? What happened?"

I fill her in on the wreck and am actually glad we have something to talk about that doesn't involve questions about my life in Boston.

"What a nightmare," she says, but then lights up. "Ooh, so does this mean you get to pick out a new car? You should see my new car. It's outrageous."

The two of us fall back into conversation as if we'd barely spent any time apart. I finish getting ready as she fills me in on everything that's been going on with our old friends and about all the cute guys who have come into town since I left.

Knox Warner's face flashes in my mind. I'm not surprised she doesn't mention him. He's definitely hot, but he's not exactly Penny's type. She only dates guys who come with a trust fund and a fast car.

"What are your plans for lunch?" she asks, then glances at her phone. "It's almost noon and I already told the girls I'd bring you to lunch at Mandy's."

I'm annoyed she already made plans for me before she even asked, but how could I say no? It's not like I have anything else on my schedule. "Sounds fun," I say, doing my best to infuse some excitement into my voice.

It's not that I don't want to see the rest of my friends. I do. It's more that I can't shake this everlasting feeling of disappointment and sadness. So far, being home has only made it worse. I feel restless and displaced. Not exactly a recipe for fun times with old friends.

I agree to go because I know I can't sit here in my room for the rest of my life. Eventually, I'm going to have to show my face in this town and hope I can figure out where I fit in after all this time. No use putting it off.

My grandmother used say 'Fake it 'til you make it.' I decide to take those words to heart as I follow Penny down the stairs and out the front door. Today, I will pretend to be the happy, smiling girl I wish I could be.

I gasp at the shiny silver sports car parked in front of my house. It looks like something from the future, sleek and gorgeous. And incredibly expensive. "You've got to be kidding me. Is that your new car?"

She flashes her bright white smile and perfect teeth. "Yes. A present from Daddy for getting straight A's last year."

I have to practically scrape my jaw off the porch. "You are way too spoiled."

"I know," she says with a giggle. "Isn't it great?"

We get into the Audi and take off toward town. I don't dare ask how much it cost, but I imagine it's probably more than a couple years' worth of tuition.

Not that her parents can't afford it. The Wrights are the richest family in town by a mile. Probably one of the richest families in the state of Georgia. Her dad owns the local factory, a business his grandfather opened in the early 1900's. Of course, the Wright's real money comes from cotton. Acres upon acres of cotton.

My parents are well off, but when it comes to money, they aren't even in the same zip code as Penny and Preston's parents.

Which is exactly why my mother nearly had a heart attack when I broke things off with Preston and decided to move away to go to school. She'd had her heart set on her little girl marrying into one of the wealthiest and most powerful families in the state. I'm pretty sure she already had my wedding all planned out since my first date with Preston at the end of sophomore year.

Maybe that's also one of the reasons she pushed so hard to get me back here.

Penny pulls up to the cafe and parks behind a blue car with a Hello Kitty for President bumper sticker. I smile, knowing that can only belong to my friend, Summer. She's been crazy about Hello Kitty since she was three years old.

"There they are." Penny points and waves furiously at a group of girls sitting on the patio.

I take a deep breath and step out of the car. Penny loops her arm in mine and practically drags me to the table.

I study them as we get closer. Krystal looks exactly the same with her long, straight black hair and perfect tan. Summer has a bright pink streak in her hair and is wearing a tight black dress with pink straps that match. There's no sign of Bailey, and to be honest, I'm relieved. The last time I spent any real time with Bailey was the night before Valentine's Day our senior year. She'd been naked and straddling my boyfriend at the time. Not that anyone knows that but me, Bailey and Preston.

I'm glad she's not here.

Summer stands and scrunches her nose, holding her hands out to me.

"You grew," I tease as I hug her.

She turns her shoe to the side so I can see her heels. "I got tired of being the short girl," she says.

"You look gorgeous."

"Thanks, so do you," she says. "You haven't changed one bit."

My heart aches at her words, but I don't let it show on my face.

Krystal stands, but waits for me to come to her. "Now come over here and grab a seat so we can roast you over the coals for ignoring us the past two years."

"I know. I totally suck," I say, taking an empty chair. "I was always thinking about you."

"Sure you were," Summer says. "Just like you were always calling and coming to visit and—"

I shove her shoulder and laugh. "Okay, point taken."

"Well, you're here now and we're dying to hear what's been going on since you left," Krystal says. "You're the only one who was brave enough to get the hell out of this podunk town. We want to hear about everything."

"Especially all the hot guys you've slept with so far," Summer says.

"Summer!" Penny slaps her hand down on the top of the table, then looks around as if she's mortified someone will hear. Then she leans in and mock-whispers, "Okay, maybe just a few sexy stories. But not so many you make us all jealous."

Nerves knot in my stomach. I wish I could laugh and tell them all kinds of funny stories about the hot guys I dated. But there's only one guy who comes to mind and there's no way I'm going to talk about him right now. Or ever.

Instead, I lie. "I know you're going to hate me, but seriously, school swallowed me whole," I say, staring at the menu and avoiding their probing looks. "My life is totally boring. I haven't had any time to really date anyone since I got there. Besides, I want to hear what's been going on with you guys. I really missed you."

That's all it takes to steer the conversation away from

myself. Over the past year or so, this is a game I've learned to play. Any time someone gets close to the truth or asks a question I can't answer, I change the subject or ask them to talk about themselves. At school, it worked fine most of the time because I never really allowed myself to get close to anyone other than my roommate Sophy.

But here? I'd been close to all of these girls once. We were like sisters back in the day.

Will they eventually see through me and want to know the truth?

I catch my mind wandering and force it back to the conversation. I smile at all the right times, laugh in all the right places, ask all the right questions. But how long will I really be able to keep up this act? It's only been a few minutes and already I feel exhausted.

After an hour, I'm beginning to wonder if I made the right decision coming home at all. It's easier to hide on a college campus where there are thousands of students. Here in Fairhope, though, everyone knows me.

Then, across the street, I see the one person in this town I only just met. And suddenly, I feel like I'm exactly where I am meant to be.

CHAPTER 7

P enny waves her hand in front of my face, and I blink and turn my attention back to her and the rest of the girls.

"Sorry, what were you saying?" I take a bite of my club sandwich even though I'm not very hungry.

"Um, no," she says. She turns deliberately and gawks at Knox across the street. "You can't spend ten straight minutes staring at some guy across the street and then pretend it's nothing. What's up?"

I tread lightly. "Do you know him?"

All three girls turn to stare at him and he notices. A half-smile tugs at his lips and even from here, I can tell he's looking right at me when he lifts his head in a nod of recognition. I want to die of embarrassment. When the others turn around, he goes back to unloading boxes from the back of his truck. I know I should look away, but every time he picks up a box, the muscles in his arm tighten against the sleeve of his black t-shirt and it does something to my insides. Plus, the guy just looks good in jeans.

"That's Knox Warner," Summer says. "He moved here probably a few months after you left."

Krystal crinkles her nose and leans forward. "Don't waste your time," she says in a mock-whisper. "Trust me on this one."

I narrow my eyes at her; a weird tightness squeezes my chest. "What do you mean? Did you guys go out or something?"

She shakes her head and her eyes grow wide. "No, are you kidding me?" She leans forward even farther. "He moved here from Chicago or somewhere like that, but he spent something like three years in jail up there for drugs and assault. I heard he practically killed some guy with his bare hands."

My mouth drops open and I carefully close it and try to hide my shock. I look over at Knox, but have such a hard time reconciling the sweet guy who was so nice to me the other night to this story about a druggie who almost killed someone. I don't buy it.

"Does he work over there?" The answer is obvious, I guess, since he's been unloading boxes for the past half hour. Still, I want to know. I want to understand why a guy like him would even move to a small town like this just to get a job at some dive bar.

"It's his uncle's bar," Penny says. "I think he works there full time to help them out and then he lives over their garage. He's a loser, Leigh. Like Krystal said, don't waste your time." She smiles and sits back in her chair, a devilish look in her eyes. "Trust me, there are much prettier boys at the college parties. You'll see."

"Oh yeah, and there's one coming up," Krystal says.

Penny shoots her a look, and Krystal's makes a face.

"What?"

"Well, there's a party next weekend to celebrate the end of finals and beginning of the summer and everything, but it's..."

Krystal's voice trails off and she looks to Penny, as if asking permission to keep talking.

"Just spit it out already," I say.

"It's Preston's party," Summer says finally.

"So?" I don't understand why that makes it such a secret. Yes, Preston and I dated for a few years. Did that suddenly mean I couldn't be near him? "He doesn't want me there?"

"No," Penny sits up and puts her hand on mine. "That's not it at all. Of course Preston would love to have you there."

The three girls share another secretive look and I want to scream. What are we? Kindergartners? "Spill it."

Penny sighs and puts a dramatic hand against her chest. "I know it's completely awkward and weird because we all grew up best friends and there's supposed to be this secret pact that you never date your friend's ex," she begins.

She's rambling, stalling, but I'm way ahead of her.

"Preston's dating Bailey," I say simply.

The three of them have such pity in their eyes. It makes me want to claw them out. Do they really think this will be devastating news for me right now?

"It's fine," I say with a shrug. I can tell from their expressions that no matter what I say, they're still going to believe that this is awful news and that I'm just pretending I'm not crushed by it.

"I should have told you sooner," Penny says, "but we rarely ever kept in touch and it just never seemed like the right time to tell you, you know?"

"Seriously, it's fine." I kind of want to tell them that I knew about Preston and Bailey long before they ever did, but I don't want to get into that right now. Instead, I'm much more interested in the fact that there are only two more boxes in the back of Knox's truck.

I set my napkin down on the table, scoot my chair back, and stand.

"Where are you going?"

Three sets of sad puppy-dog eyes stare up at me. Poor Leigh Anne. They have no idea that Preston's betrayal is nothing compared to what I've been through since.

"I need to run across the street, real quick," I say. "I'll be right back."

I don't give any more explanation than that before I leave the patio, look both ways, and cross the street.

CHAPTER 8

Knox pauses and watches as I cross the street toward him.

I'm hyper aware of how I look. How I walk. I try not to smile like a silly girl as I get closer. I also try to remind myself that he probably thinks I'm a lunatic. Or a bitch. And probably wants nothing to do with me.

"Hey." He's sweating out here in the Georgia heat and lifts his shirt to wipe the sweat from his forehead. I catch a glimpse of toned abs and my breath catches in my throat.

"Hey," I manage, forcing my eyes to his.

Which isn't much better. Turns out his blue eyes are just as blue in the light of day.

"How are you feeling? Any soreness in that shoulder?"

"It's a little worse today, to be honest." I reach over and massage the area between my neck and shoulder. "I'm hoping it's just temporary."

"You really should get it checked out."

I'm touched by his concern. He's been nothing but ultra-sweet to me, and I'm just not able to believe he would hurt

anyone on purpose. Whatever story Krystal heard, it was probably dumb, trumped-up rumor mill bullshit.

"I'll probably give it a couple of days," I say. "I hate
hospitals."

I have my reasons.

He nods and squints in the bright sunlight beating down on
him. "Me, too."

I stare down at my feet, wondering again how to express my
gratitude for what he did the other night. "I wanted to thank
you again," I say. "And I wanted to apologize."

He lifts his head and adjusts his baseball cap. "For what?"

"For all of it," I say with a laugh. "For having to carry all my
junk. For crying all over you. For the way my mother treated
you."

He crosses his arms over his chest and leans back against
the side of his truck. "Yeah, she wasn't too friendly," he says.
"We can't control who our parents are, though. You don't ever
have to apologize for her. And the rest of that stuff? I didn't
mind it at all."

He looks at me and I see there's something haunted in his
eyes, too. Something I didn't see the other night, but that
flashed, deep down, when he mentioned parents. Something I
recognize because it's exactly the same expression I see in my
own eyes when I look in the mirror. He's been hurt by someone
just like I have, and I wonder if it's the kind of thing you only
recognize when you've been there yourself.

I want to ask him about it. Tell him I see it and I know
what it's like. But that would be crazy, right?

Besides, if we start sharing secrets it'll open up a whole can
of worms I'm not sure I'm ready to open.

He stares across at my friends, then looks down. "Your
friends are staring at us like they never saw two people talking
before."

I turn to look and the three of them all look away. Busted. I laugh. "They're nosy."

"I recognize a couple of them from around town," he says. "I think that girl with the pink hair has been in the bar a couple times. You guys been friends a long time?"

I nod. "Since we were kids," I say. "Most of us were born and raised here, so we all grew up together."

"But you don't live here anymore?"

I hesitate. What's the real answer to this question? My parents decided it would be best for me to come home for the summer, but I fully planned on going back to school once the media coverage dies down. Now that I'm here, though, it's hard to think about going back.

"I'm in transition, I guess." A gust of wind blows my hair all around my face and I gather it up in my fist and hold it back.

"Well, what I was getting at was whether you planned on sticking around here for a little while or whether you were only here a few days," he says.

The question sparks fresh tingles along my skin. "I'll be around all summer."

He smiles with his eyes. "That's good news," he says. He clears his throat and shifts his body weight from one foot to the other. It's the first time I've seen him look anything less than perfectly confident since we met. "I was hoping maybe you'd let me take you out to dinner or something one of these days. If you have the time."

I want nothing more than to break out in a full smile and say hell yes, but something holds me back. Maybe it's that haunted look I saw earlier. There's something there that tells me I could trust this guy. I could really let down my walls around him.

Which is exactly why I need to walk away.

Besides, I don't need to go pulling him into the mess that is my life right now. Even if I am attracted to this guy, where could it possibly go? Nowhere, that's where. So what's the point?

I push any potential happiness deep down and reach for my standard excuse instead. "I wish I could," I say, "but it's really not a good idea."

He doesn't say anything at first. He studies me instead.

"Why are you staring at me like that?"

"I'm trying to decide if you really aren't interested or if you're just trying to protect yourself," he says.

His words hit way too close to home and a lump forms in my throat. I swallow it down and take a step back.

I'm not used to people being so direct with me. I'm used to passive aggressive bullshit.

"Maybe it's you I'm trying to protect," I say.

His eyebrows tense, then release, and he shakes his head. "Why would I need protection from you?"

I take another step back and shrug. "Because I'm like that windshield the other night," I say. "All broken pieces and sharp edges."

"That doesn't scare me," he says.

I laugh and shake my head.

"It probably should," I say. "I'll see you around."

I cross the road back toward my friends, and even though I don't dare look back, I can feel his eyes on me the whole time.

CHAPTER 9

My phone is ringing.

I run up the stairs and practically dive across my bed to reach it in time.

I'm expecting a call from Penny with plans for a trip to the lake tomorrow. Only, it isn't Penny. Caller ID reads Sophy and in an instant, it all comes back to me. I lay my head down on the comforter and close my eyes for a second. I've been home for almost a week and Mom was right, it's been getting easier and easier to slip back into my old routines and my old life.

And everything that happened at school is getting easier to ignore. I can't forget it, but it's one of those out-of-sight, out-of-mind things. The moment I see her name on my phone, though, I'm thrust right back to that place.

I debate whether to ignore it or pick up; when it stops ringing. I breathe a sigh of relief and place the phone back on my nightstand. Before I get off the bed, though, it starts ringing again.

Knowing Sophy, if she has something important to talk about, she won't stop calling until I pick up.

I lie back across the bed.

"Hello?"

She sighs. "Thank God," she says in her smooth British accent. "I was beginning to get really worried. You know I've called about half a dozen times since you left campus?"

Guilt rushes through me. I've seen the missed calls, but largely ignored them. Not because I don't like Sophy. I adore Sophy. She's one of my best friends in the whole world. But she's also one of the only people in the world who know the truth. "I'm sorry," I say. "It's been an adjustment being home."

"I bet," she says. "I don't know how you can stand living in a town where the most exciting event of the year is a watermelon harvest."

I laugh and roll my eyes. "It's not that bad."

"Seriously, tell me how you're holding up," she says. "Is your mom being nice to you?"

"I'm actually enjoying the quiet," I say. "It's nice to get away from the media circus on campus, anyway."

"But you're coming back, right? The media will get tired of Molly's story eventually," she says. "I think."

I swallow. I don't know what to say. Am I going back? The truth is it's more than just the whole Molly thing that makes staying at school difficult. Even before she came forward with her story, I still had to see him every once in a while. Running into him on campus when I least expected it was the worst part of it all. The way he'd sometimes look at me and smile, like we shared some secret joke. Or worse, the way he'd walk right past me without even glancing my way, like nothing had happened between us at all.

"I don't like this silence," she says. "Leigh Anne, don't tell me you're thinking about staying in Georgia?"

"Why not?" I sit up. It's not the most ridiculous idea in the world.

"You can't just quit school halfway through," she says. "What will you do? You can't honestly be thinking of transferring."

I think about how Knox said he wasn't the college type. Maybe I wasn't the college type either. "I'm thinking of not even going back to school for a while."

"Don't be ridiculous," she says. "You're way too brilliant to quit."

I shake my head. I'm the opposite of brilliant.

"I don't know what I want to do." I pick at the corner of my pillowcase. "I only just got here. We've got months until fall semester anyway."

"I know," she says. "I just don't want you to think you need to hide out down there forever. Don't let him win, Leigh Anne. You're stronger than that."

I close my eyes and lay back against the headboard. Am I strong? I don't feel strong. I feel beat-down. Exhausted. So tired of this mental fight with myself.

"We'll see," I say. "I'm going to take it one step at a time and try to enjoy the break. It's really nice here in the summer."

"Liar," she says, and I can hear the smile in her tone. "It's a hundred and eighty degrees there or something outrageous."

I laugh. She's right, but I don't give her the satisfaction. Besides, today it's only a high of ninety-seven.

"I miss you," I say.

"Then pick up the phone every once in a while, okay?"

"Deal."

"I miss you, too, by the way," she says. "Summer school's not the same without you."

We say our goodbyes and hang up, and for the rest of the day, my mind is stuck in Boston with her. And with the memories I left behind.

CHAPTER 10

"Leigh Anne, are you coming? We're going to be late for our reservations." My mother calls up to me and I quickly check my makeup in the mirror one last time. I'm not sure why I care so much. I don't even want to be with Preston anymore, but I still want to look good when I see him for the first time in almost two years. I mean, this is the first guy who made me feel butterflies. The first guy to take me all the way.

And now he's dating the girl I caught him cheating with.

I need to look good when I see him.

"I'm coming," I shout. I grab the black clutch from my bed and run down the stairs to meet them.

My father is wearing a black suit and for the first time, I notice how gray his hair has become. He looks so much older than I remember, and I wonder what life has been like for him over the past couple years. Has he been working too hard? I know there have been some problems at the factory lately, but I haven't really paid attention to the details. I make a mental note to spend less time obsessing over myself and spend some time really catching up with him.

He smiles and opens the door for me. He's such a gentleman, and I can feel his love for me radiating from his eyes. I feel bad for staying gone and just before he closes the door, I reach out to touch his hand.

Our eyes meet and I give him a small smile. He leans over and kisses my forehead, just like he did when I was a little girl.

"We really should hurry," Mother says. "I told Andrea we'd be there by seven and it's almost five minutes after."

As if Andrea really gives a shit that we're late. Andrea, my mother's sister, is probably already three drinks deep at the bar. Still, I keep my mouth shut rather than disagree with my mother tonight. Better not to stir things up.

As soon as the car pulls onto the street in front of our house, my mother angles toward me in her seat and starts in on the questions.

"How was your day at the lake with Penelope, sweetheart? I have really missed seeing her around the house since you left," she says.

I smile obediently even though it's dark inside the car. "We had a great time," I say. The truth is I was bored almost the entire time. I love Penny, but the more time we spend together, the more I realize how much distance there is between us. We don't really care about the same kinds of things anymore.

It's the same with all my old friends. I'm not sure I really fit in with them anymore.

"Who else was there?" she asks. "Did you get to see anyone fun from the old gang?"

Gang. As if we are a wild group of thugs wreaking havoc all over town instead of a set of six rich girls who never do anything we aren't told.

"Most of them," I say, deciding to test what she knows. "Bailey couldn't make it, though."

I watch her face carefully. Does she know Bailey has been dating Preston?

Her lips press together briefly, and I instantly know that yes, she knows about Preston's new girlfriend. And she has no plans to tell me about it. "That's a shame."

Dad pulls up to the valet and a guy I recognize from high school opens the door for me. I know we graduated together, but I'm completely blanking on his name, and for some reason, this really bothers me. It's like there's some kind of black hole where my memory used to be. Not that I was his best friend or anything, but it's not like it's been twenty years. It's only been two.

How could I have lost touch with everyone so quickly?

He smiles and says hi, so I smile too and tell him it's nice to see him again. He takes my father's keys and drives away with a smile on his face and hopefully no idea I can't place him.

I smooth the skirt on my green dress and my father offers his arm to me as we walk up the marble stairs toward the entrance. We've been here a thousand times, but tonight I'm nervous. I know Preston will be here with his family, and I wonder if Bailey will be with him. It shouldn't matter to me at all, but it does. I can't explain it.

Maybe it's some kind of territorial thing. He was mine for so long, it's hard to imagine him with someone else. Or maybe it's the secret I carry about his relationship with Bailey when we were still together. Was he in love with her back then? I'd always thought it was only about the sex between them.

The thought of there being something real between them leaves me feeling empty and sad.

I decide to dust off my pageant smile and plaster it across

my face like armor. Just in case. If they are here together, I don't want either of them to see that it bothers me.

The doors open and the gold and crystal chandelier in the foyer sparkles in the light, welcoming me back. Straight ahead, the dining room is bustling with people. It's a normal Friday night with all of Fairhope's most influential families in attendance, drinking their cocktails and getting into everyone else's business.

I remember thinking how fun it was, when I was a teenager, to get all dressed up and come to a fancy place for dinner, but now? I have a sudden distaste for this whole scene.

Nothing's changed. Nothing but me.

I try to take a deep breath, but the stuffy air chokes me.

I'm nervous about running into Preston. Or rather, nervous about running into him and Bailey. I can already picture her hanging all over him like an old coat. I wonder if her expression will be one of guilt or pride.

The fact that she's been avoiding me since I came home suggests guilt.

The hostess shows us to the same round table near the window where the Davis family has sat for more than a decade. I'm not surprised to see that Aunt Andrea isn't even here yet. After a brief phone call, Mom announces her sister isn't even going to make it tonight. Typical.

We sit down and peruse the menus, pretending we'll order something exotic or different when everyone knows that Dad will order the steak and Mom will have the salmon.

My choice always used to be the chicken parmesan with broccoli and a side salad, and even though I consider trying something new, when the waiter comes, my old order comes tumbling out of my mouth almost without a thought. I guess old habits die hard. Or maybe I just want to feel like the old me tonight.

I hand the waiter my menu, then freeze as I see him across the room.

Not Preston.

Knox.

Suddenly, the breath is knocked from my lungs. I have to remind myself to breathe in before I pass out. He is the last person I ever expected to see here tonight.

He's standing at the bar with a beer bottle in his hand. He's leaning over, talking to the bartender and laughing.

Instead of his typical uniform of t-shirt and a baseball cap, he's wearing a button-up shirt. No hat. His hair is longer on top than I thought. Dark, with the slightest hint of wildness.

The jeans are the same.

There's something about Knox Warner that makes my temperature rise about ten degrees. I shrug the sweater from my shoulders and place it on the back of my chair.

The bare skin above my strapless dress feels warm like a sunburn.

All this, just from being in the same crowded room as him? I know it's insane. Maybe I'm crushing on him so hard because he held me as I cried and didn't ask for anything in return. Or maybe I just like the way his jeans are tight in all the right places.

Either way, I know he's nothing but trouble. My life is already incredibly complicated. The last thing I need right now is a summer romance.

Still, I can't help looking over my glass of water to study him again. He's got this casualness to him; a laid-back sort of sense of self. Confidence. Like he couldn't give a shit what anyone in this room thinks of him.

And in this particular room, that was saying a lot.

He downs the beer and sets it on the bar. As he turns to go, his eye catches mine. My heart jumps into my throat, and my hand jerks, nearly spilling my water all over the table.

My mother shrieks as a few drops spill onto her gold beaded purse. She snatches it out of the way and clucks her tongue. "Leigh Anne, watch what you're doing."

"I'm sorry," I say, pressing my napkin over the tiny spot of water.

By the time I look up again, Knox is gone. Disappointment floods through me. I search the dining room, but there's no sign of him anywhere.

"Leigh Anne?"

I hear my name and turn my attention to the person who just appeared at my side. My mouth falls open. "Preston."

He's alone.

I stand and we hug.

"Wow," is all he says at first. His eyes travel from my head to my toes. "You look amazing," he says. "It looks like the big city agrees with you."

My throat is suddenly dry as a bone. I quickly take a sip of water, then force a smile. "You look great, too," I say.

He does look good. Better than good. The same, but older. More mature. But looks can be deceiving. No one knows that better than me.

"It's been a long time," he says, sadness crossing his features. "Penny told me you were home, but I guess I needed to see it to believe it."

I don't know what to say, so I stay quiet, and an awkward silence falls between us.

"Leigh Anne is going to be here all summer," my mother says, her voice just a little too happy. "Maybe even longer, if we're lucky."

I want to kick her for saying that. There's been no decision about whether I'm staying and it feels like a betrayal that she would discuss that in public. My angry look is lost on her, though. She's staring up at Preston like he invented water.

"Is that true?" He studies my face, but I can't read his expression at all.

"I'm not sure," I say. "We'll see how the summer goes, I guess."

It's a dumb answer, but I wasn't expecting to have to answer questions about going back to school.

Preston shoves his hands into the pockets of his expensive navy suit. "I should probably get back to my table before they order without me," he says with a laugh. "It's really great to see you, Leigh. We should catch up."

"Sure," I say. "It's good to see you, too."

He lingers until I look up and our eyes meet. I wait for the butterflies to come.

Only, they never do.

CHAPTER 11

I wake up feeling restless.

I'm struggling to try to fit in here. To forget and move on, but all of a sudden, the thought of spending today with old friends makes me sick.

The few times we've all gotten together, I've had brief moments of fun, but mostly I'm just bored. I don't know the people they're always talking about from school. I don't care about the same high-school style drama they're still living in. Plus, it's getting harder to avoid questions about my own life. Sooner or later, someone is going to catch on and start asking tougher questions.

I need something new to take my mind off it all.

After a few hours of playing mindless games online, I finally go searching for my mom to see if she needs help in the garden or around the house. Not surprisingly, I find her sitting at the kitchen table flipping through yesterday's newspaper. She has her usual cup of coffee in front of her and offers me a cup.

I shrug, pour myself a cup and sit down. "I need something to do," I say. "Do you need help with anything?"

"Why don't you call some of your friends? I'm sure they'd love to spend as much time with you as they can while you're home," she says. "You could always go to the mall or go for some ice cream. Just like old times."

"We're not fifteen years old anymore, Mom. Most of them are in summer school or have jobs, anyway." I pick up a section of newspaper she's discarded and see a listing for help wanted.

I sit up straighter. I could get a job. I'm not sure why I didn't think of it sooner. I've never actually had a job before. My parents have always had plenty of money, and as long as I kept my grades up, they were always giving me enough money to do the things I wanted to do. Plus, I dated the richest guy in town all through high school.

In college, there simply wasn't time.

But now, why not? It's the perfect way to spend my summer. It'll keep me busy and give me an excuse.

I lean forward and start scanning the listings, searching for anything that looks remotely interesting. Something fun where I can make good money and meet people my own age, but something busy so I won't have time to think.

There are a few ads for secretarial work and entry-level positions in places like the hospital, but none of them sound very interesting. Then I see the perfect thing. The local steak house, Brantley's, is looking for servers. I fold the paper so that the listing is right in the middle, then stand up, leaving my untouched coffee on the table.

I grab the keys to my new car off the rack near the back door.

"Where are you going?" my mother calls after me.

"I found something to do," I say just before the screen door slams behind me.

IT'S ONLY TEN IN THE MORNING WHEN I GET THERE AND Brantley's isn't open yet.

I pull on the outside door, but it's locked. I frown and peer through the glass doors. I look at the ad again and see that they don't list a certain time to stop by. Maybe I came too early?

I walk around the side and notice a few cars parked toward the back. I decide to go around back and just see if there's anyone here. A heavy-set woman sits on a picnic table behind the restaurant, smoking a cigarette. She looks up as I approach and nods toward the paper in my hand.

"You here for the waitress job?"

I nod. "I tried the front door but it's locked," I say. "Should I come back later?"

I'm pretty sure I recognize this woman, but her name won't come to me. Martha? Something like that.

"You're here, ain't ya? Might as well go ahead and interview. I'm Maria," she says. "What's your name?"

"Leigh Anne Davis."

She squints up at me, the skin around her eyes and forehead wrinkling. "Leigh Anne Davis. I remember you. Haven't seen you around much for a few years, though. Didn't figure you for the type who'd come looking for a job like this."

"I've been out of town for a while," I say, not bothering to explain where I've been or how long I'm planning to stay. "I could really use a job, if you're still hiring."

"You got any experience?"

I bite my lip and shake my head. "No, but I'm a fast learner."

She raises an eyebrow and tosses her cigarette down to the pavement. "I bet you are."

I'm not sure what she means by that; if it's meant to be a compliment or an insult.

She pushes herself up from the table and turns her back on

me, disappearing through the back door. I shake my head and toss the piece of newspaper onto the table. That didn't exactly go as planned. Maybe getting a job was a stupid idea. People in this town already have an idea of who they think I am. They still see me as some prissy rich girl, but that's not who I am. Not anymore.

I turn to go when she sticks her head back through the door and yells, "You coming, or what?"

"I thought the interview was over," I say, completely confused.

"It is," she says, then smiles. She's missing a tooth along the top, but her smile is contagious and full of joy. She knows she's messing with my head and she's loving every minute of it.

"I don't get it," I say.

She laughs, then waves me inside. "Come on in, girl. You're hired."

She disappears around the corner again, but leaves the door standing open. I shake my head, then with a smile, I follow her inside.

CHAPTER 12

"Where in God's name have you been all night?" My mother's voice is so wound up, I half expect her to start spinning in circles. "I've called you five times."

"I texted you to say I would be gone all day," I say, not wanting to tell her about the new job. I know she'll be angry, which is stupid because most parents would be proud of their children for getting a job. My mother will say it's beneath me to wait tables. And she'll worry about how it will make her look in town.

That's all she ever cares about.

"That still doesn't tell me where you've been, young lady."

Young lady. I'm still a child to her. It's getting harder and harder to hold my tongue around here.

Instead of talking back to her, I just don't answer. Instead, I walk past her, up the stairs and into my room. She doesn't follow me.

I strip my clothes off and toss them onto the floor, then start the shower. I turn it up so it's really hot. As hot as the dish water at the restaurant, steam billowing up. I need to wash the stink of the food and the smoke from my body and my hair. I need to feel something.

Ever since I got back here, I've felt disconnected. At least back in Boston, I knew where I stood. I was used to the routine up there; and even though my heart was in chaos ever since Molly Johnson's face first appeared on the front page of the campus newspaper, at least I had daily access to what was going on.

Here, I am on an island.

No one understands me or knows what I'm going through. Everyone thinks I'm the same old Leigh Anne, and the fact that not one person has noticed a difference makes me feel even crazier. How can something so monumental not leave any noticeable scars? How can I walk around feeling raw and bare and not have one friend recognize it?

Today was the first day home that I felt useful instead of lost.

Maria hired me right away, then put me to work washing dishes all night. I barely had two seconds to talk to anyone or even go to the bathroom, but the best part was that I didn't have any time to think either.

Despite my aching feet, I'm looking forward to going back tomorrow.

When I get out of the shower, my phone is blinking with a new message. I turn it on and see Preston's number there for the first time in years.

Hey. Really missed you. Party at my place this weekend. 212 Allan Street, apt 4A.

I lay back against my bed, processing. I don't even know for sure how I'm supposed to feel about Preston. When I left Fairhope the summer after graduation, I thought of him all the time. Catching him with Bailey broke my heart and I was all mixed up about it for months. Sometimes I wondered if I'd made the wrong choice going away to school instead of staying behind and trying to patch things up between us.

Over time, though, it stopped hurting so much. I met new guys at school and started dating again.

Of course, that didn't have a happy ending, either.

I don't know what to think now that I'm home. He seemed happy to see me the other night, but if he's really been dating Bailey this whole time, why is he sending me a message saying how much he's missed me?

I probably shouldn't go. It will just confuse things.

On the other hand, all my old friends will be at that party. If I don't show up, they're going to wonder why I'm avoiding them. And if I keep avoiding them, eventually they'll stop calling all together.

If I'm smart, I'll find some way to slip back into my old life instead of running from it. Become the old Leigh Anne everyone seemed to love so much back then. If I can figure out a way to be like her again, I'll be safe. I'll have a future here.

It sounds so easy, but really, it's the hardest thing in the world.

My phone buzzes again and I see Preston's number flash on the screen a second time.

Come. Please.

My heart twists. I'm more confused than ever. In some ways, I'm glad to be home again. I want to find a way to fit in and be carefree the way I used to be. In other ways, though, I miss the independence I had in Boston. There, I had my own place and made all my own decisions. I didn't feel like people were watching and judging my every move.

Right now, I'm not sure who I am anymore or even who I want to be.

The only thing I am sure of is that whatever I decide, I need to be careful. No matter where I go, the road is paved with emotional landmines. All it will take is one wrong step and everything I've been holding in for so long will come bursting out of me.

No matter what, that's the one thing I can't allow to happen.

CHAPTER 13

"This your first day?" A short girl with her hair pulled into two uneven pigtails comes to stand beside me.

I set the stack of trays down beside the washing station and wipe my forehead. "Technically, I guess it's my second day. How could you tell?" I ask. "Surely it can't have anything to do with the fact that I've been stuck back here washing dishes for the past two hours?"

Sweat rolls off my skin and my hands are raw from the heat of the water.

The girl laughs and leans against the large industrial sink. The collar of her white shirt pulls down slightly and I can see part of a tattoo that runs along her collarbone. She's chewing gum, which I'm pretty sure is against the rules. She doesn't seem to care.

"This is Maria's version of a hazing ritual," she says. "She makes all the new blood wash dishes at first. I think it's her way of judging someone's character or something like that."

She pats me on the back and sets her tray on top of the pile. I hold back a groan.

"Don't worry," she says. "Tomorrow night she'll only make you do an hour of dishes, tops."

My eyes go wide and the girl giggles like my agony is the funniest thing in the world.

"Don't look so serious. I'm only joking," she says. "I'm Jenna, by the way."

"Leigh Anne." I don't offer her my hand because it's disgusting and wrinkled and covered in pieces of discarded food.

"Maria asked me to train you. Have you ever been a server before?"

I shake my head and wipe my forehead again.

"It's not that hard," she says. "It's all about time management. Once you've been out there a few days, you'll start to get the rhythm of it. Come on, why don't you take a little break. Do you smoke?"

I glance toward Maria's closed door. She's in there with some guy I'm pretty sure is the owner. "I don't think I have permission to take a break yet."

Jenna laughs and grabs my arm, pulling me away from the dishes and out the back door. The sun has gone down and a nice breeze is blowing. I lift my face toward the wind, grateful to be out of the heat of the kitchen for a second.

Jenna pulls a pack of cigarettes from her apron and offers one to me. I wave it off. She shrugs and lights up.

"So, where you from?" she asks me as she sits on top of the picnic table.

"Here, actually." I join her, so glad to be off my swollen feet for a few minutes. Maria's had me working all day long, cleaning up, reading the employee handbook, washing dishes. I am exhausted and in a weird way, it feels really good.

"How come I've never seen you before? The town's not that big."

"I graduated a couple years ago and went away to go to college. I just got back," I say.

"So you're just home for the summer?"

I'm not sure how to answer that question. "Maybe. My future's kind of up in the air right now."

She nods, but doesn't press me for more information.

"What about you? How long have you been here?"

She takes another drag of her cigarette, then blows the smoke away from me. "I moved here last summer," she says. "Transferred to FCU from a junior college in Macon. I'll be a senior this year. I'm so ready to be done with school."

FCU is Fairhope Coastal University. It's a small school, but one of the best in the state. "What are you majoring in?"

"Sex and drugs," she says, totally deadpan. Then, she breaks out in laughter. She throws her cigarette to the ground and stomps it with her boot. "No, seriously though, I don't do drugs."

She walks back into the restaurant, then turns and winks before disappearing inside.

A laugh escapes my lips, and it's one of the first times in a long time that it's real.

"Wait," I call after her, feeling impulsive. She stops just inside the door and waits for me to catch up. Thinking of Preston's party, I ask, "What are you doing Friday night?"

CHAPTER 14

I park in front of Preston's apartment building and sit in the car, watching. The parking lot is completely packed.

I'm late. Work was insane tonight. I shadowed Jenna the whole time and I don't think we stopped for a break for five straight hours. I took a shower when I got off and rushed here as fast as I could. Jenna said she'd meet me here and that she might bring some friends from the restaurant.

It's almost eleven already and I've had two texts from Preston asking if I was still planning on coming.

For a second, I think about driving away. Maybe I will just keep driving until I leave the Fairhope city limits. I could disappear, change my name, start over.

I get out of the car and walk up to the apartment. He's on the fourth floor and it isn't hard to find the right place. The door is open and music is thumping. Even my shoes are vibrating.

"Leigh Anne!"

I turn just as a rush of pink hair streaks toward me and

slams into me. Summer. She's drunk and stumbling. Ice cold liquid drips down my back as she hugs me.

"Hey," I say, hoping she's drinking something clear. I have to raise my voice for her to hear me over the music and the crowd, even though we're technically still in the hallway. "Sorry I'm late."

"Hey, bitch, where you been?" A guy with spiked blond hair approaches and holds his hand up to me, waiting for me to reciprocate.

I lift my hand and he squeezes it, then gives me a one-armed hug.

"Hi, Mason, what's up?" Penny's crush and Preston's best friend. For the last year of high school, I hardly ever saw the guy without a drink in his hand. From the looks of it, nothing's changed.

"I'm serious, where in the world have you been hiding? I haven't seen you in forever."

"She's been at school, dumbass," Summer says, smacking his arm. "She's home for a month or something."

"Cool. It's good to see you," he says. He glances back inside. "You want a drink?"

I press my lips together. Do I?

"You always were way too serious. It's not a test question or anything," he says with a wink. "Just a simple yes or no."

"Get her one of these," Summer shouts, pointing at her red cup.

I have no idea what's in there, but from the way she's slurring her words and tripping over her own feet, I know it's strong.

But I don't say no.

Summer wraps her arm around mine and we squeeze through the packed living room toward the kitchen where

Mason is making me some concoction of vodka and rum and juice. He smiles and hands it to me.

"Here you go, Princess," he says. "You want me to let Preston know you're here?"

I take a drink and nod, even though I'm not sure I'm ready to see Preston yet.

I figure in this crowd, it could be a while before he finds me, anyway.

With our fresh drinks, Summer pulls me out toward the dance floor where we meet up with Penny and Krystal.

They both throw their arms around me and scream with excitement.

"Where the fuck were you?" Penny shouts over the music.

"At work," I shout back.

Her head flinches back and she squishes her eyebrows together. "What?"

"Work," I say again.

She shakes her head and looks at me like I've lost my damn mind. "Why are you working? I thought you were on summer vacation?"

I shrug and down my entire drink in one shot. I'm so tired of this divide between us. Why does there always have to be all this judgment? Shouldn't friendships be about just being yourself around each other, no matter what?

At the same time, I know they aren't the ones who are acting strange.

It's me. I'm the one who's changed.

I throw a glance toward the front door, but there's no sign of my new friends. Who knows if they'll even bother to show up?

Tonight, all I really want is to have fun for a change. Let loose and just be a part of the crowd again. I'm tired of feeling so fucking alone. Maybe if I keep drinking, I can forget what happened in Boston long enough to remember who I was before it happened.

Fuck it. Why not?

I see Mason standing in the doorway leading to the kitchen and catch his eye. I hold my empty cup up and point to it. He nods, then turns back toward the kitchen.

I take Summer's drink from her hands and down that one too. She pretends to be pissed, then kisses me on the cheek and laughs. Penny takes my hand and pushes it high into the air with an excited scream I can barely hear over the music.

And just like that, it's old times again.

CHAPTER 15

Preston finds me in a sea of drunken college students and I'm well on my way to being one of them. The drink in my hand has been refilled three times, and I have no idea how long I've even been here. It has to be well past midnight.

His arm wraps around my waist and before I know it, I'm dancing with him. The music is fast and hot, but we're going slow, his body pressed against mine. I beg my body to feel something. To find that old attraction to him. To want him again like I used to.

I don't know why I want to want him. Maybe because life with him was easier. A guy like Preston could protect me and when I was with him, people looked at me like I mattered.

"I'm glad you came," he says in my ear. His breath is hot and he reeks of whiskey. Even the most expensive whiskey still smells like gasoline when he's been guzzling it.

"Nice place," I half-shout over the music, even though there are way too many people here for me to tell what the hell this place looks like. "I'm surprised your parents let you off their leash long enough to get a place of your own."

He laughs. "I didn't even bother asking. I just left."

I smile, but I know he's lying. Preston gets his dad's permission before taking a piss too far from home.

"You look so good, Leigh." His fingers brush the bare skin at my waist, exploring the space between my tank top and the band of my jeans.

I want to shiver, to burn, but I can't force myself to feel anything.

"So do you," I say, pretending I still feel it. I want to feel it.

He buries his face in my hair. "God, I missed you so much."

I let him pull me close, but my eyes are scanning the crowd behind him. A few people are looking our way, but it's Bailey's eyes that are burning into us. I meet her stare and guilt flares through me.

It isn't fair for me to come back here after all this time and take him back.

But it wasn't fair for her to fuck him when he was mine, either.

I look away and put my arms around his neck, drawing him closer. The room spins. I close my eyes and concentrate on the familiar form pressed against me. Preston was my first. My first kiss. My first love. My first heartbreak.

His body knows mine better than anyone else.

I expect to feel more for him, but even with the alcohol spinning around inside me, I am numb.

And it makes me want to push some boundaries.

He pulls back just enough to look into my eyes. "Want a private tour?"

Of course, I know what he means by that and I'm surprised he's moving so fast. Especially since the girl he's been dating is standing less than twenty feet away. Has it even

THE TROUBLE WITH GOODBYE

crossed his mind that he should care about how this makes her feel?

Probably not.

He takes my hand without waiting for a response and guides me toward the back hallway. People greet us with smiles and shouts as we pass. Familiar faces mixed with strange new ones. I play the part of Preston's girl. It's a part I played for so long, it comes naturally.

The apartment is much bigger than I expect and the hallway feels endless. Finally, he opens the door to his bedroom and guides me inside. He closes the door and the noise is muffled, leaving a ringing in my ears.

For the first time in hours, I can hear myself swallow.

And I'm nervous. Uncomfortable, even. What the fuck am I doing? Do I really want this? I can't think straight.

"I can't believe you're really home." He stands a few inches from me and studies me like it was his job, his eyes taking in every inch of my body. "It's like you're a ghost."

I laugh at his choice of words. A ghost is exactly what I feel like here. Someone who died a long time ago.

"Come sit with me."

I obey him because that's what I do. That's what Leigh Anne Davis has always done. She obeys. She doesn't have a mind of her own. She doesn't like to rock the boat. She's meant to look beautiful and do as she's told. A cardboard cut-out of a real human being. Nothing more than an easily manipulated prop.

When I tried to be something more, I got hurt. Maybe this version of me is the best one, but I don't know how to get back here.

My head is swimming.

He sits on the large king-sized bed and motions for me to join him. I go to sit next to him, but he pulls me onto his lap instead. I'm straddling him and his breath grows shallow. I place my hand on his chest and his heart is beating fast.

He grinds himself against me.

This is supposed to turn me on. I'm supposed to want him right now. What the hell is wrong with me?

Fear tenses my shoulders. I understood my indifference with the guys back at school. I could rationalize my lack of desire, telling myself these guys just weren't the right kind of guys.

But Preston? He used to be the love of my life.

If I can't make myself feel something for him, I'm more broken than I thought.

I thrust my fingers into his hair and pull his lips toward mine. I part my lips and he devours me. I pretend it's affecting me and let his hands roam over the top of my clothes. I moan, faking it, hoping that at any moment, this will all become real. I pray this will be my time machine. That one kiss will somehow erase the pain. I want to be the old me. The girl who used to love Preston Wright and who rocked in pleasure at the feel of his lips on her skin.

He stands, lifting me up from the bed. In one swift movement, he flips me onto my back and is on top of me. An unexpected panic floods through me and I struggle for breath.

I was fine when I was the one in control, but now the power has shifted and I feel claustrophobic.

I push up on his chest and try to get some air, but he takes it as an act of passion and presses harder, crushing me beneath him. His mouth is covering mine and I can't breathe. I scratch at his clothes and turn my head to the side, but he's too drunk to notice. He moves his mouth across my jaw line and down my neck, but the weight of his body is like an anchor pulling me under.

This isn't what I want.

"Stop, please," I say, but the words sound weak. The sound

of my own voice scares me, and I suddenly think I've been here before. That it's happening all over again.

I gasp for air, my pulse racing.

Preston doesn't even hear me. He pushes his fingers down past the waistband of my pants and a bright light of anger and fear pulses through me. With every ounce of strength I can gather, I push and kick. I grab his wrist and pull.

Finally, I scream. "Get the fuck off me!"

He freezes. His eyes fly open and for the first time, he looks at my face. Tears well up in my eyes and spill down my temples and into my hair.

His eyebrows draw together and he pulls away, awkwardly taking his hand from my pants.

I scramble backward on the bed. I've gone too far. Made a complete fool of myself. And I have no idea how to explain it. This is my ex-boyfriend. A guy I've had sex with a hundred times. And I just completely freaked out when he tried to touch me.

I don't blame the confusion I see on his face.

"What the fuck just happened?" He doesn't sound angry, just dazed. He stays at the end of the bed and makes no move to come closer.

"I'm sorry." I draw my legs up close to my body and hug them tight to me.

I search for a good explanation. Anything that will keep him from asking too many questions.

"I'm trying to figure out what just happened here," he says. He stands up and runs a shaky hand through his hair. "Did I misread you? Or is this where we were headed?"

"I don't know. I thought I wanted this," I say.

"But you don't?" he asks, his face tense. I've hurt him. Wounded his ego.

My hands are shaking. "I don't know what I want," I say, but that isn't exactly true. I want impossible things. I want to erase pieces of my past. I want life to be easier. I want everything to be okay.

"I think I should go." I scoot off the end of the bed and head for the door.

Preston touches my hand "Wait."

"I'm really sorry I freaked out." I wipe tears from my cheeks. "It's not your fault."

I know Preston would never do anything to hurt me. I led him on, kissed him like I wanted him, and then screamed bloody murder all in the space of about five seconds.

But I can't stay and explain why. Not to him. He wouldn't understand.

I apologize again, then open the door and disappear into the crowd.

I don't look back, but I don't think he's following me either. A few familiar faces say hello and try to pull me into conversation, but I make quick excuses as I rush by. I need to hold myself together just long enough to get out of here. I'm about two point five seconds away from a major meltdown and I really don't want anyone to see that. Not here. Not tonight. Please, God, just get me out of this stupid party.

It was a mistake to come here.

I push and smile and worm my way through the crowd, run down four flights of steps, then finally break free. The humid night air brushes against my cheeks and I can breathe again. Fresh tears hover at the edge, just waiting for the floodgates to open. I hold them back. I've cried too damn much lately.

But like my tears, I'm a girl on the edge. I hover at the top of some great height, peering over the side into nothingness. If I step back, I might lose myself forever. But one inch forward and I'm fucked. It's fly or die.

And in this moment, I'm just not sure I'm the flying type.

CHAPTER 16

I pull my car keys from my pocket, but as I unlock the door and sit down, I realize I've had way too much to drink. Even though I feel stone-cold sober, I know I can't drive right now. The last thing I need is to total a second car. Or to get pulled over. I rest my head against the steering wheel.

I'd rather die than call my parents and ask for a ride home. Penny and the other girls are all still inside the party, and there's no way I'm going back in there.

I have no idea if Jenna and her friends ever even made it.

My choices are to either sit here until I'm sober enough to drive or walk.

I get out of the car and lock the doors. It's got to be at least five miles to my parents' house, but I don't care. I need to move my feet. I need to blow off some steam and try to get my head on straight.

I acted like a complete asshole tonight. All it will take is a couple more nights like this and the whole town will be talking about what a mess Leigh Anne Davis has become. People will figure it out. They'll know, and they'll start asking questions I don't know how to answer.

My mother will never let me hear the end of it, either.

I can't live like that. I have to hold it together.

I step onto the narrow sidewalk and slip my heels from my feet. I should have worn flip-flops, but I wanted to look sexy. Pretty stupid after a night of waiting tables. My feet are swollen and a blister is already forming at the edge of my pinky toe.

I make it fifteen minutes into my walk of shame before the first tears begin to fall. I'm honestly surprised I made it that far.

A few cars pass by, but I don't look up. I hope it's no one from the party, because I look like an idiot walking home like this. I really hope it's no one I know.

And then I notice someone has slowed down and is matching my pace. I keep my eyes forward, but I know they are still there. If it's Preston, I am going to die.

Finally, I give in and look.

It's Knox.

My mouth opens slightly and I suck in a ragged breath. I quickly swipe at the tears on my cheeks and laugh at my luck. This is the second time he's seen me cry, and I don't even want to think how crazy that must make me seem. How weak and drama-queen and high-maintenance.

I stop and he stops too. The windows on the beat-up truck are rolled down and he's got one arm leaning out the driver's side, but he's ducking his head slightly to look at me through the passenger side.

"I thought that might be you," he says. "You need a ride?"

I look forward as if calculating just how far I still have left to go. "No, I'm fine." I try to smile. "Thanks, though."

I give him a slight wave, then start walking again. I expect him to wave back, maybe say goodnight, and keep moving.

But he doesn't.

I stop again and sort of cock my head and raise an eyebrow, questioning. "Are you planning on following me like this all night?"

"Well, the way I see it, it's two in the morning and that's not really the best time for a pretty girl to be walking all alone, even in a small town like this," he says. "You didn't run your car into another tree or anything right?"

I roll my eyes, but I smile. "No, I just..." My voice trails off. For some reason, I have the urge to really open up to this guy. I want to tell him all about my night and how badly it sucked. And for some reason, I feel like he'll understand. Like he'll get it.

Maybe it's something about those clear blue eyes and the flash of sadness I saw in them before. He's been through hard times, and I know it somehow, even though I barely know him at all.

"You just felt like taking a leisurely walk through town in the middle of the night?" He says it with a slight smile on his face, and I smile again too, then duck my head to try to hide it.

"Well, what about you?" I ask. "What, do you just drive around town every night looking for damsels in distress so you can play the hero?"

He raises his eyebrows. "Maybe," he says. "I do make an awfully good hero when given the chance."

I can't hide my smile now.

"Get in," he says. He leans across the seat and pulls the handle on the passenger door, then pushes it open. "I'll take you home."

I shake my head. "I'm not sure I want to go home right now," I say. My mother is probably waiting up for me, even though I'm twenty years old. I can't face her right now. Not like this. Plus, I still can't shake this anger and confusion. "I really need to just blow off some steam. It's been kind of a rough night."

"Well, it just so happens I know the all-time best way to blow off steam."

I laugh, then bite my lip. I'm torn. For reasons I can't explain, I really want to get into this truck with him.

But is that stupid? I literally just freaked out when my ex-boyfriend tried to make out with me. Is getting in a truck with a complete stranger so he can take me lord-knows-where really the smart choice here?

I look up and he's staring at me with a world full of patience in his eyes. It's almost as if he understands the weight of the choice I'm making and he respects it.

I think of the way he held me that night in the dark. He pulled me into his arms without a second thought and never questioned my pain. I think of the butterflies I feel every time I'm near him. Butterflies I tried to force with Preston just to prove I'm still alive. That I'm not broken.

Only, the truth is, I am broken.

And the guy right here in front of me is the only one who sees it. For some reason, he seems to like me anyway.

I think maybe what I've been doing wrong this whole time is chasing my past and hating myself for not being that girl anymore. Maybe what I should do instead is learn how to embrace who I've become.

I think I'm over-analyzing this whole thing.

I stop thinking, and I get in.

CHAPTER 17

Knox drives and I lean my head against the door and let the wind whip my hair across my face.

He drives through downtown and keeps going. We end up on Harrison's road, passing the scene of my accident. I don't ask where he is taking me. For me, it's an exercise in conquering fear. Learning to trust my instincts again.

After another minute, he stops in front of an aluminum gate and hops out of the truck. He quickly unlocks the chain and drags the gate open, then gets back in.

We're surrounded by endless woods and the night is dark except for his headlights and a distant moon that lights the treetops.

The truck bumps along the rugged dirt road that winds through the pine trees. I'm not exactly sure where we are, but I know we're near the lake. A few of my friends have houses near here.

We turn a corner and a house comes into view. I don't get a good look at it, but I do notice a blue tarp covers one side of the roof. There are black marks like scars against the white paint near the roof and windows. Signs of a fire. In the darkness, it's hard to tell the extent of the damage.

"What is this place?" I ask.

"This is my dream house," he says.

I'm not sure if he's joking until I look at him and see the excitement in his eyes. He's completely serious.

I look at it again with fresh eyes. I can see the potential here, maybe. I want to get a closer look.

"Show me," I say.

He opens the door for me and I take his hand as he helps me down. The simple contact sends shivers up my arm.

I leave my heels in the car. He leads me to the small screened-in porch at the back of the house. It's very dark now, without the truck's lights, but he bends down and turns on a camping lamp. He lifts it up like we're explorers in some kind of cave and we enter the old house together.

"Watch your step," he says, pointing out a burned piece of wood on my left. "Stay on this side."

"What happened here?" I look around and see the beauty of this place. It's older than I realized at first. There's a lingering scent of smoke, but I can also smell the heart-pine of the floors. An archway still stands between this back room and the kitchen, but the rest of the house on that side is ruined. The detail of the woodwork that survived, though, is breathtaking.

"Kitchen fire," he says. He shakes his head and stares at where the kitchen once stood. "About ten years ago."

"It's just been sitting here empty this whole time?"

He leads me down the central hallway where a large staircase leads up to the second floor. "Yeah. My uncle didn't really have the money to put into fixing it," he says. "I hate to see it like this, though. My grandfather built it when he first got married. My uncle and my mom both grew up here. That's part of the reason I decided to move down here. I thought I'd try my hand at fixing it up myself."

He runs his hand along the railing.

"My mom really loved this place," he says.

"Does she know you're fixing it up?" I ask.

He shakes his head and there's a sadness in his eyes. "My mom died from cancer when I was fourteen."

A heavy feeling settles in my stomach. "I'm so sorry."

"The house has some really beautiful bones to it," he continues, but I can tell he's a bit shaken up from talking about her. "Just look at these banisters. All of this was hand-carved by my grandfather. I think it's worth saving."

I stare at the way his hand runs so gently across the top of the wood. There's such love in his touch. Such passion.

He must miss her with all his heart.

I am struck with the desire to place my hand on top of his, and I look away, swallowing hard.

He shines the light up toward the ceiling. "See the old bead-board ceilings? You don't really see that kind of work and craftsmanship anymore. It's really cool."

"It is."

Only, I'm not really looking at the ceiling. I'm looking at him, thinking how this is the last place in the world I expected to end up tonight.

"What?" he asks, lowering the light. "You think I'm crazy for trying to save all this?"

"No." I shake my head. "I was thinking how crazy it is that I'm here at two in the morning with a complete stranger looking at an old burned down house. This night has been so... strange."

"Well, I didn't really bring you here to see the house," he says, a smile lighting up his eyes with mischief. "We came here to blow off steam, right?"

He grabs my hand and leads me through the front door and out onto the porch.

My eyes widen. The large wrap-around porch looks straight out to the moonlit lake. It's so beautiful out here, it takes my breath away.

He sets the light on the porch and lets go of my hand. Immediately, I miss the warmth of him. He walks down the steps and begins pulling his shirt up and over his head. Even in the dim light of the moon, I can see the ripple of muscles in his arms and back and my breath quickens.

Just what exactly does he have in mind?

He turns, walking backwards with a glint in his eye. "Come on, then," he says, tossing his shirt to the ground. He reaches for the buckle on his belt and my heart skips.

The buzz from the alcohol has long since faded, but there's a new buzz starting deep in my belly and it makes me light-headed. I haven't felt this way in a very long time. Maybe ever.

I follow him to the edge of the lake. At first, I think we're heading toward the dock and I suddenly realize he means for us to go swimming. But he turns and disappears into the woods, surprising me again.

"Where are you going?" I ask, laughing and shaking my head. He's the most wonderfully surprising guy I've ever met.

Seconds later, his blue jeans hit the ground at the edge of the trees and the fire in my belly spreads lower. I'm not sure I'm ready for this, but I'm not sure I want to leave either.

There's a tiny voice inside that tells me to panic. To run.

But there's a louder voice that says this guy is different. He gets me somehow. And he has never once pushed me or made a move toward me that felt rushed or uninvited. I stare down at his discarded clothes and wonder just what in the world he has planned.

I hear rustling in the trees, then Knox shouts as he flies by, holding tight to a rope that swings out over the mirrored water. He lets go and before he hits the water, his eyes meet mine. I laugh and bring my fist to my lips, not sure I've smiled so freely in months.

He disappears beneath the surface for a moment, then breaks up, shaking the water from his head.

"Well?" he shouts.

"Well, what?" I shout back.

"You coming in or what?"

The rope is still swinging at the edge of the water. I eye it, bouncing slightly on my toes, unsure what to do. I've never been the impulsive type. I'm usually the girl who plans everything, which is probably why I have such a hard time when things go wrong.

"I don't think I can," I say, scrunching my nose. I want to, but it's so ridiculous. Swimming in the lake in the middle of the night?

"Why not?" he asks, laughing. He's treading water, and I'm glad there's almost a full moon tonight. Otherwise, I'm not sure how well I'd be able to even see him out there. "What are you so afraid of?"

"I'm not afraid," I say, but I'm lying. I'm terrified. Not of the water or the rope. I'm terrified of what I'm feeling for him and how perfect he seems to be. I don't deserve this. I don't know what to do with this.

"If you're not afraid, then what the hell are you waiting for?"

The sadness I've been carrying around for so long urges me to take a step back, away from the edge of this mountaintop. But there's a growing hope that tells me to seize this moment with both hands.

What the hell *am* I waiting for?

Breathless, I jog toward the woods, slip out of my jeans and toss them to the side. I reach out for the swinging rope, catching it on its second pass toward the shore. There are several tight knots and I grip the highest one with two trembling hands. I back up the hill until the rope is taut, and with my heart beating fast, I hold on tight.

And I fly.

CHAPTER 18

I am half screaming, half laughing when I hit the water. It's freezing cold, but there's no turning back now. I slip under, then swim toward the surface. When I break free, I am new. Reborn.

Knox makes a whooping sound that echoes across the lake and I splash him with a wave of water.

He splashes back, then swims toward me fast. I screech and try to swim away, but his hands slip around my waist and pull me back until my body is pressed close against him. Our faces are inches apart. Under the water, our legs move in unison to keep us afloat. It's the perfect kissing kind of moment, and I realize I want it.

Bad.

He draws his bottom lip into his mouth and bites. His hand gathers the edge of my tank top into a fist and his fingers brush the bare skin underneath. This is nothing like the way I felt when Preston touched me. Was that really just a couple of hours ago?

I know I should pull myself together. Ask him to take me home. But I can't move. All I can do is stare at his lips.

He breaks away, nearly dunking me as he swims back toward shore.

"Where are you going?" I ask after him.

He pulls up on the edge of the dock. "Again."

I smile and swim after him.

We jump and swim and play for what seems like hours. We're like kids on a summer's day. Only it's the middle of the night. And the way he makes me feel is not something I ever felt as a kid.

Exhausted, we both collapse on the dock and lean back, staring up at the night sky. I haven't laughed this much in ages. We're both breathing heavily, our chests rise and fall and our arms lie close against the wood. Not quite touching, and so very aware of it. The moon is nearly full tonight and the stars are out in force.

"I haven't seen stars like this in years," I say finally.

He brings an arm up under his head and inches the tiniest bit closer to me. "Yeah, you don't realize how much you miss it until a night like this," he says. "It's impossible to get views like this in the city."

"Did you grow up in the city?" I wonder again about Chicago.

"No, I grew up in a place a lot like this, over in Alabama," he says. "I moved to Chicago when I was ten, though. No stars."

"That had to be shell shock at that age," I say, thinking of how long it took me to get used to the Boston area when I first moved away for school.

"You have no idea," he says.

I want to ask more, but I don't want to spoil our night with questions about the past. I like this feeling of being right here, right now, fully in the present.

His hand brushes against mine, and my mouth goes dry. My lips part and I swallow, my breath short. I feel his eyes on me, but I'm scared to turn and face him. After all my begging to feel something, anything, I'm afraid when it finally happens.

But this fear is a different kind of fear. It isn't filled with panic and terror or with a desire to run away. What I'm feeling is a strong pull toward him. Pure desire.

The space between us is electric and I'm aware of his every breath, every movement.

Finally, I give in. I turn my head toward his. Our eyes meet and I shiver. We both lift up at the same time, our legs dangling off the edge of the dock but not quite touching the water. His hand comes up to caress my cheek and his skin on mine sends a rush of warmth through me.

He moves toward me slowly, our eyes locked together until the very last moment, when they close and we surrender ourselves to touch.

I'm breathless as his lips find mine. At first, there is only softness, an inhaling. Time stands still and I lose all sense of anything but the pressure of his lips and the growing flush of heat in my core.

His fingers tense against my jaw and I lean into him. He exhales, his breath warm against my skin. His tongue teases my bottom lip and I open slightly, letting him taste me. Tasting him back.

When he pulls away, my heart is racing so fast, I can barely keep myself from trembling. I'm increasingly aware of the fact that we're both in our underwear, but he makes no move to push me further. He keeps his hand placed firmly on the spot where my neck and jaw meet. He leans his forehead against mine and exhales, a smile teasing the corners of his mouth.

"God, I like you so much," he says in a whisper.

I smile and reach up to put my hand on his wrist. "I like you too."

It's such a simple confession, but it's real and honest. I want to sit here with him all night. I want to kiss him again, but the sun chooses just this moment to start peeking over the horizon.

He runs a finger along my temple, tracing a tiny scar. "What happened here?"

I break away and turn to look at the pink and purple coloring the sky at the edge of the lake. I close my eyes and my shoulders fall. I don't want to talk about that. "I need to get home," I say.

We're still holding hands as we walk over to our discarded jeans. I'm completely under his spell and wish this night could last forever. I don't want to go home and have to answer to my parents, but I know it's inevitable.

We dress and get back in his pickup truck. We don't say much the whole ride home, but the farther we get from the lake house, the more the magic of the last couple hours fades away. He asks me if he should drop me off at my house, but I give him directions to Preston's apartment complex instead.

"You never did tell me why you were walking home tonight," he says.

"Bad party," I say. "I'd had a couple drinks and didn't want to risk driving home, but I just had to get out of there. It was a rough night."

He nods.

"It got better," I say, cheating a look at him.

"The party?" he asks, his eyebrows cinching in the middle.

"No," I say. "My night."

He smiles and reaches over to take my hand.

I want to ask if I'll see him again, but now that the sun is coming up and reality is sinking back in, I'm confused and torn in two directions. I really like him, but he doesn't need for me to drag him into my mess. And the closer I get to someone new, the harder it will be to keep secrets. Until I can be sure I'm ready to talk about what happened up in Boston, I can't really allow myself to start something new. It wouldn't be fair to either one of us.

Still, I want him. There's no denying it. Is it stupid to push him away?

"Thanks for the ride," I say when we get to the parking lot.

"It was my pleasure."

I place my hand on the large metal handle of the old truck. "I'll be sure to look for you next time I'm stranded in the middle of the night," I say with a laugh.

He leans forward against the steering wheel. "I was hoping maybe we could see each other sooner than that."

I press my lips together and close my eyes. I don't know what to say to that.

"I really did have fun tonight," I say. My heart is aching because I want to be free and tell him that yes, let's see each other tomorrow and the next day and the next. But at the same time, I am still chained to my past. I can't afford to get hurt right now.

"But?" he says.

I shrug. "But my life is really complicated right now."

He studies me. "Maybe that's why you should just say yes," he says. "Sounds to me like you could really use more nights like tonight."

I can't help but smile. He's definitely right about that. "The problem is that nothing stays fun and carefree like this forever," I say. "Once emotions get tangled up inside it, everything becomes complicated. And I can't afford another ounce of complicated right now.

His face falls and he swallows hard. "Whatever happened to you, I wish I could take it all away."

The words sink deep into my heart and hot tears spring to my eyes. "It doesn't work like that," I say, my voice barely a whisper.

"I know," he says. "Doesn't make me wish it any less."

We sit there, a heavy silence between us. I feel the weight of the words I wish we could say to each other. Words we might share in another place, another time, if things weren't so complicated. If we both hadn't been through so much that wanted to stay buried.

I grab my high heels from the floorboard of the truck and open the door. "Good night, Knox," I say.

"Good night, Leigh Anne," he says back.

I still feel our connection tugging on me as I step onto the pavement.

It lingers long after I've gotten in my car and driven away from him, wishing I'd had the courage to say yes.

CHAPTER 19

My mother's voice echoes across the hardwoods and I jump.

"Jesus, you scared me to death." I turn and find her sitting in the formal living room. It's a room we never use and I know she's only there because she can see the street from here and she's been waiting for me.

There's a book open in her lap and she's wearing her glasses and a long pink robe. She's not wearing any makeup and I can't remember the last time I saw my mother without her armor on.

"Leigh Anne, it's six in the morning," she says. "Do you have any idea how worried I've been?"

I start to apologize, but then I remember I'm not sixteen years old anymore. I'm twenty. "I'm not a child anymore, Mom," I say. "I don't have to tell you every time I go out, and I don't have to be home at any certain time. I'm sorry you waited up for me, but I can take care of myself."

"Can you?"

The look on her face is harsh and angry, and I know exactly what she means by those two little words. She blames me for what happened in Boston. She blames me for leaving Preston. A responsible, capable woman would never let such things happen.

Anger boils up within me, and I clench my teeth together, holding back the things I want to say.

"Where were you?" She pulls her glasses off. "I know you weren't with Preston."

I stare at her. I'm not even going to ask her how she knows I wasn't with Preston. I'm too mad to engage in this conversation.

"I'm going to bed." I walk toward the stairs.

"Don't walk away from me." She stands and raises her voice.

I turn but don't say anything. I'm afraid of what might come out if I speak.

"You may not be a child anymore, but you still live under my roof, which means you live under my rules," she says. Her anger wrinkles her face and makes her look older than her fifty-three years. "You cannot go off for hours without even telling us where you are. Did you know that I had to hear it from Janine that you've gotten a job at Brantley's? Really, Leigh Anne? What on earth possessed you?"

"What possessed me to get a job?" I ask. "Why do you act like that's such a bad thing? People have jobs, Mom. Not everyone gets to be a social butterfly who never has to work a day in her life."

She lifts her chin. "It's not the job that bothers me, it's the fact that you kept it a secret."

"I knew you would act like this if I told you," I say. "You're always questioning my decisions these days, like you think you know better or something. I need to be able to make my own choices."

"You did make your own choices," she says, pointing her finger wildly. "Look where that got you."

Her words are like a punch in the gut. I was right, she does think it's my fault. I'm so hurt, I don't even want to look at her right now.

"I'm tired," I say, turning away. "I'm going to bed."

I make it halfway up the stairs before she says my name.

I don't stop, and I don't look back.

CHAPTER 20

My phone rings too early. I roll over and shield my eyes against the bright sunshine streaming in through the windows.

I squint at the caller ID and groan. Sophy. I decline the call and cover my head with a sheet.

A minute later, the phone rings again. I think about throwing it across the room, but sit up instead. I look at the missed call log and see it's the fifth time she's called already this morning. Er, afternoon. It's already one. I decide to answer the phone. If she's called this many times, something's up.

I take a deep breath, preparing myself for bad news.

"Hi, Soph," I say. "I was sleeping."

"It's one in the afternoon," she says.

"I'm aware. I was up late."

"Well, I'm glad you answered the phone." The relief in her voice is evident. "There's something you need to see."

"What?" My stomach dips.

She sighs. "Turn on the news."

I reach over to my nightstand and grab the remote. I turn

on the small flat-screen on my dresser and flip channels until I see it.

Her.

I watch as Molly Johnson is ushered into a black car. She's wearing sunglasses and putting her hand out in front of the cameras.

My eyes travel to the ticker along the bottom. *Redfield case takes a turn. Johnson admits to lying about assault in high school.*

I feel nauseated.

"What is this?" I ask, pulling the phone back up to my ear. "What are they talking about, an assault in high school?"

"Apparently Molly accused some guy of sexually assaulting her in high school," Sophy explains. "She later turned around and said she was lying about it."

I close my eyes, my heart shrinking inside my chest. I can't speak.

"Leigh Anne? Are you okay?"

I swallow and take a deep breath. "I don't know."

"I'm sorry to surprise you with this, but I didn't want you to be going about your day and find out from someone else or right in the middle of something," she says.

"What does this mean? For the case?"

She clears her throat. "It's not good," she says. "The media is crucifying her over this. If she lied once, she must be lying again, that sort of thing."

My head falls heavy into my palm. I want to lie back down and crawl under the covers for the next forever.

"I'm sorry," she says again.

"See, I told you something like this would happen. Especially with all the press involved," I say, not lifting my head. I can't feel my feet or my hands. There's a ringing in my ears. "This is why it's easier to just keep it locked inside. When you come forward with something like this, suddenly your life is ammunition against you. Every bad choice. Every moment you ever took a breath."

"When did you ever make a bad choice?" she asks, her voice soft.

I collapse further onto the bed. The phone is pressed so tightly against my face.

"The day I agreed to go on a date with Burke Redfield."

CHAPTER 21

After the news, I want to stay in bed for days, but it's my new job that gets me into the shower and out of the house.

The TV over the bar at work is usually set to sports, but of all nights, tonight they have it on CNN. Every time I leave the kitchen, I pass by and catch a glimpse of Molly Johnson's face. Or worse—his face.

The news media is all over this case and every time I think about it, I want to run to the bathroom and puke up my lunch. It's such a weird sensation to see something playing out on television and know that there are only a few people in the whole wide world who know I'm a part of it. I go back and forth between hating the whole thing and wishing I was brave enough to speak up.

I'm staring at the TV again when Jenna comes up behind me and loops her arm through mine. She follows my gaze up toward the screen. It's too loud in here to actually hear what's going on, but the closed caption is on and I can read some of it as it passes by. The press is looping her story, saying she's a serial liar. A mentally unstable girl looking for attention.

And what better target than a drop-dead gorgeous movie star?

My stomach turns and I grind my teeth together so hard my jaw aches.

Jenna rests her head on my arm. "That girl is so incredibly brave," she says. "Can you imagine? Every piece of your past, every mistake you ever made, being paraded around as proof that you're a liar just because you accused some rich boy of hurting you?"

Her words bring tears to my eyes. I want to hug her and tell her I love her for saying that. For taking Molly's side despite the recent news. And I want to tell her that yes, I can imagine it. I have imagined it every day for the past year and a half. Instead, I just say, "I could never be that brave."

"Me either," she says.

I reach out and take her hand. Just knowing I might not be the only one too scared to face something so horrible makes me feel better.

"Hey." She squints up as the name of the school flashes across the screen. "Isn't that where you go to school?"

I swallow and try to look disinterested. "Yeah."

"That's so crazy. Did you know her?"

I shake my head. "Not really," I say. The truth is I've never met Molly Johnson in person, but in some ways I think I probably know her better than most people. I know how something like this changes you. I know how brave she is, and how, despite what they're saying, I know she's telling the truth about Burke Redfield.

"What about him? Is he really that good looking in person?" she asks. "Did you ever see that one movie—" She snaps her fingers, trying to come up with the name.

"Indecision," I say, knowing which movie she's talking about. It's the one everyone talks about when they talk about Burke.

"Yes," she says. "That's the one. He looked so hot in that. Shame he turned out to be such an asshole."

"Don't you two have tables waiting?" Maria barks. "You can watch TV on your own time."

"Sorry," we say in unison and head back to our work. For the rest of the night, I force myself to avoid the bar area and eventually, someone changes the channel.

CHAPTER 22

 My feet are killing me from hours of standing at work. I am in serious need of a new pair of shoes. My old sneakers are just not going to cut it.

Jenna says she knows the best place in town for work shoes and texts me to meet her downtown Saturday afternoon before our shift.

I drive in and park on the street in front of a place called Punk. Not exactly the kind of place I expected to shop for shoes, but I'm trusting her. I check my phone again out of habit before I get out of the car. I keep hoping to hear from Knox. We exchanged numbers after our swim, but that was a week ago now.

Preston, on the other hand, has texted me every day. He's still trying to make sense of what happened between us the other night in his bedroom, and I still don't have any good answers for him.

Jenna's waiting near the entrance and she waves as I get out and cross the street toward her.

"Hey. Thanks for taking me under your wing," I say. "I'm clueless."

"If you keep working in those worn out shoes, your feet are going to have blisters the size of watermelons." She laughs and tugs on the door.

"Have you been waiting tables a long time?"

She leads us toward a wall of Doc Martens. "Ever since I was sixteen," she says. "So, yeah, five years now I guess. How pathetic is that?"

I don't think it's pathetic at all. She's so sure of herself. Independent and confident. "Not as pathetic as never having had a job at all."

"Are you kidding me? I wish I didn't have to work," she says. She picks up a pair of black boots that match the ones she's wearing. "What size?"

"Seven."

She bends over, pulls out a box of sevens and hands them over. I sit down on the bench and pull my old sneakers off. The shoes fit and I take the obligatory test walk through the store before declaring them perfect.

"It's gonna take a few nights to break them in and they're kind of pricey, but trust me, it'll be so worth it."

I go up to pay for them when the bell over the door rings. I don't pay attention at first, but Jenna jabs her elbow into my side and I turn to see what she's all worked up about.

I gasp and nearly drop my wallet. Preston is standing in front of me with a gorgeous bouquet of pink tulips. He looks out of place among all the leather and spikes.

"What are you doing here?"

He smiles and walks toward me, holding the flowers out. "I stopped by your house first and your mom told me you were heading here," he says. "Sorry to interrupt you guys, but I can't stop thinking about you, Leigh. I needed to see you."

Great. He's been by my house. That means my mother knows he brought me flowers. I'm sure it's made her whole week.

I take the flowers and can't resist inhaling the light scent of them. My favorites. "You remembered."

"I remember everything."

His words should make me swoon, but I know better. Preston has always been so good at the apology. It's an art form with him, really. Every time he messed up and got too drunk to remember or ended up in some other girl's arms, he always brought me flowers or bought me an expensive necklace or took me to some fancy dinner. One time he even cooked for me. Yes, he is very good at apologies.

And until Bailey, I was very good at accepting them.

"Can we talk about the other night?" he asks, then glances at Jenna. "In private?"

I want to laugh. If he wanted to talk to me in private, he shouldn't have brought flowers to a clothing store.

I look at Jenna and she shrugs.

"I don't mind," she says. "I need to stop by a friend's first anyway. I'll catch you at work?"

"Sure," I say. "Thanks again for the help with the shoes."

"Work?" Preston's eyebrows are tight, confused, as if he can't imagine why anyone would ever have to work.

I walk toward the front door, flowers and shoes in hand. "I'm waiting tables at Brantley's."

"Why?"

It takes everything in me not to roll my eyes. "I was bored."

He seems to get this as a reason. Anything is better than saying I need the money or just wanted to work to feel good about myself. He would never understand either of those things. But being bored is understandable. It makes me want to strangle someone.

Is this really the kind of person I used to be?

"I can think of other ways for you to pass your summer," he says. He smiles with only half of his mouth. It's his naughty smile. That smile used to kill me.

It isn't working today, and he knows it.

"What's wrong, Leigh? Did I do something to piss you off?"

We leave the store and walk down Main Street.

I search for a reason that will make sense to him. Something easier than the truth. "Penny told me about Bailey," I say.

His shoulders slump and he goes into explanation mode. "I like Bailey. She's a lot of fun and with you gone, she's, I don't know, someone to help me pass the time." He steps in front of me so I'll stop walking. He lifts my chin so he can make sure he has my absolute attention. "But you're the one, Leigh. You've always been the one for me. I've missed you so much."

There's something genuine in his eyes I wasn't expecting. Does he really mean that? I search his face, but I think this moment is real and it knocks the wind out of me. Why does it make me feel panicked?

"Didn't you miss me?" he asks. "Didn't you even think about me at all while you were gone?"

"Of course I thought about you." And it's the truth. Freshman year, I couldn't stop thinking about him. Then I met Aaron. And PJ. And John. After a few casual dates, I started to, not forget exactly, but to have distance.

"I thought maybe..." He releases my chin and looks away.

"What?"

"I guess when Penny told me you were home, I thought maybe you'd come back for me," he says. A sad smile crosses his lips, then fades. "Then when you actually showed up at that party, it was like old times again, you know?"

"I know."

We start to walk again and this time, his hand keeps bumping mine.

"So what happened?"

I wish I had an explanation for him.

"I don't know," I say. "I guess a part of me thought maybe we could pick up where we left off, but when you kissed me..." I shrug, unable to finish my sentence.

He grabs my hand and I don't pull away. The truth is I know Preston would be a great future for me. He's good looking, he cares about me, and he's rich. He's exactly what everyone expects for me.

So why can't I make myself want him?

"I'm sorry I got so angry," he says. His thumb caresses my index finger. "Will you go out with me? Just give me one night."

We reach the end of the street and pause on the curb. He faces me and runs his hand along my arm.

I've missed the tallness of him. His confidence is comfortable, like he could just wrap his arms around me and pull me back into the past where I was safe. Where I was still whole instead of these broken pieces of myself.

"What about Bailey?"

He shakes his head. "I don't love her."

I look up. Does that mean he still loves me? I'm not even sure what we had before was really love.

"I don't know," I say, pulling my hand away. "We'll see how it plays out, okay?"

"What does that mean?"

I take a step back. "It means I'm not sure what I want. I'm in a very strange place right now."

He steps forward and places both of his hands on my shoulders, pulling me closer. "One date," he says. "Just give me a chance to show you how things could be with us. Let me remind you how things used to be."

I close my eyes and remember. His warm, familiar lips kiss the top of my head. We've stood like this a thousand times and suddenly I'm sixteen again and life is much simpler.

But when I open my eyes, it's still today. Now. And everything we had back then disappeared a long time ago.

The low sputter of a truck idling at the stop light causes me to jerk away. My heart twists into a knot as I turn, praying it's not Knox. I don't want him to see me standing here like this with Preston.

The truck next to us is red, not blue and relief floods through me. It's not him.

But the fact that I care so much gives me the clarity I was searching for. Preston is my past, but if there's even one small chance Knox is my future, I need to at least give him a real chance.

I can only hope it isn't too late.

CHAPTER 23

Jenna pounces on me the second I walk through the back door at Brantley's.

"What the shit?" Her eyes are wide. "Are you dating Preston Wright?"

I groan. She follows me around the corner to the small set of lockers. I put my purse and phone inside and pull out my apron.

"We dated for a few years back in high school."

Her mouth drops open. "My mind is blown," she says, then smacks my shoulder. "Preston Wright is the hottest guy in town. You've been holding out on me."

I make a face and she won't let it go.

"What?" She smiles. "Tell me."

"I don't think he's the hottest guy in town," I say, then bite my lip. I haven't talked about Knox out loud to anyone. Until today, I haven't really wanted to admit it as a thing. But it's definitely a thing.

"Well, well, well. Aren't you just full of interesting surprises tonight," she says. She leans against the dingy cinder-block wall, then holds a hand out. "I'm waiting."

I step closer to her and look around to make sure no one else is listening. "Do you know a guy named Knox Warner?"

She looks up, as if searching the ceiling for him. She shakes her head. "No, I don't think so," she says. "He lives here in Fairhope?"

"Yes, he moved here probably about the same time you did, but he doesn't go to your school or anything," I say. "He bartends over at Rob's."

"Oh, yeah, I know that place. I went there once to play pool with Colton after work." Her mouth drops open again. "Hot bartender! I remember him."

My insides get warm just thinking about him, but then dread fills me up. "I think I ruined it though."

"What happened?"

I'm considering how to explain our midnight swim when Maria comes around the corner, her eyes all squinty.

"We're going," Jenna says, rolling her eyes. "Slave driver."

Maria smacks her on the butt as she passes and Jenna giggles. Just before she heads out into the dining room, she turns to me and raises her eyebrows. "After work tonight," she calls out. "You and me. Rob's."

I lean against the wall, enjoying the butterflies.

CHAPTER 24

Country music escapes as the door to Rob's opens. The guy leaving holds the door open and tips his hat to us. Jenna raises her hand to an imaginary brim and tips her hat back at him. He winks at her and keeps a keen eye on her ass as she walks in.

A fact, I think, not lost on Colton. He gives the guy a look and waits for him to keep moving until he follows us to an empty booth.

I haven't spent much time with Colton, but he seems like a cool guy. He bartends for us at Brantley's, and I've noticed Jenna lingering up there during her shifts lately. She hasn't mentioned anything about dating him, but if it hasn't started yet, it won't be long.

I wasn't expecting her to bring him tonight, but Jenna grabs my hand and insists my secret is safe.

"I'm very good at keeping secrets," Colton says with a wink. "Comes with the job description. So, who are we here to stalk?"

"The bartender," Jenna says. She props her leg under her

butt so she can sit higher and searches the bar area. "I don't see him."

"I have no idea if he's even working tonight," I say. "I haven't even talked to him in a week."

"Wait, are we talking about Knox?" Colton asks.

The concern on his face worries me. I hope this isn't going to be more of the Chicago rumor bullshit.

"Yes, why? Do you know him?" Jenna asks, leaning in.

Colton raises one eyebrow. "I've seen him around, but he's kind of known for being notoriously hard to get."

This is news to me, and I'm not sure what to make of it.

"How so?"

Colton shrugs. "When he first moved down here a year or two ago, all the girls flocked to this place, checking out the new guy," he says. "I used to hear a lot of chatter about him from the girls at Brantley's."

"And?" Jenna motions impatiently. "Spill it."

"He never goes out with anyone," he says. "He comes to work, he does his job, he keeps to himself. That's the rumor anyway. For a while, I think some of the girls even had a running bet about who could get him into bed first."

My mouth goes dry. I'm not sure I want to hear the rest of this.

"No one ever won as far as I know," he says. "None of them could even get him to go out on a date. Then it got out that he got into some kind of trouble up in Chicago. Drugs or fights or something, who knows. The girls at work declared him an asshole and moved on, I guess."

Asshole is not a word I would ever associate with Knox. To me, he's been the sweetest guy in the universe. I can't reconcile it in my head, which only makes me doubt myself. Lord knows I've made some bad choices.

Am I totally misreading him?

"Well, how do you know him, then?" Jenna asks, turning to me.

I hesitate. I haven't even told anyone about my car accident or what happened at the party that night. I don't even know where to start or how much to tell. "The night I came back into town, I almost hit a deer. Smashed my car up pretty bad," I say, having to practically shout over the music. "He saw my car and stopped."

I don't mention the fact that he carried me from the wreckage or held me while I cried for thirty minutes, but thinking of it sends a warmth through my middle.

"He's a hero in disguise," Jenna says, nodding. "I like it."

I glance toward the bar, hoping to catch sight of him. Instead, I recognize a girl from high school behind the bar. Joey Young. Well, Josephine, but everyone's called her Joey since she was five. We used to be friends in first grade when we had to share a desk, but when we got older, our relationship turned sour. I still don't understand what happened there. It was like with the flip of a switch, suddenly Joey hated me for no reason. No logical reason, anyway.

I watch her making drinks and am amazed at how fast she slings the bottles and gets the drinks on the bar. She's wearing a black tank top that shows off her flat stomach and the tattoos on her arms. Those are all new since I left town.

Someone comes to stand next to her behind the bar and she looks up and smiles. I follow her gaze and my heart skips a beat. Knox is laughing and whispering something in her ear.

Jealousy washes over me until I put two and two together and remember that if his uncle owns this bar, then that means Joey is his cousin.

My shoulders relax. I would hate to be in competition with someone like her. The girl's got attitude.

Of course, that didn't bode well for my having a relationship with Knox, either. Not if they are really close. I twirl a strand of hair around my finger. Crap, what if that's part of why he hasn't called me?

Maybe she feels my eyes on them, but right at that moment, Joey looks up. Her eyes cut straight through the crowd to me. She turns, shouts something at Knox, then nods toward me. He glances my way, and I'm like a deer in headlights. I know I should look away, at least try to pretend I wasn't staring, but I can't. I'm frozen.

"Is that him?" Jenna asks. She stands up and follows my eyes toward the bar.

I'm mortified because now my whole table is staring at him.

He catches my eye across the bar and like a moron, I lift my hand in the most pathetic little wave. He smiles and looks down at his feet, then cuts his eyes back up toward me.

I thank god I'm already sitting, because my knees go weak.

I tear my gaze away only to see Jenna fanning herself. I grab her hands, so embarrassed my cheeks flush.

"He's fucking hot," she says. "I say go for it."

Colton shifts uncomfortably, and I laugh. I wonder if Jenna even realizes how hard he's crushing on her. If she does, she's playing it super cool.

I, on the other hand, am the opposite of cool.

"So, how exactly do you think you screwed this up?" she asks.

I touch a palm to my forehead and grimace. "He asked me out and I said no."

She collapses against the back of the booth and pretends to faint, falling toward Colton with the back of her hand raised to her head. He gladly catches her and she opens her eyes. "Why would you do that? When was this?"

"Last weekend," I say. "Hey, did you guys ever show up at that party by the way?"

"No, we didn't make it," Colton says. They share a look that has me very suspicious about the current state of their relationship.

"Uh huh," I say, studying her.

She makes a face, then raises her eyes to the ceiling, as if she has no idea what I mean. I remind myself to ask her about this when we're alone.

"Well, it happened the night of the party," I explain.

"If you like him, why would you say no?" Colton asks. "Women are so weird sometimes."

Jenna punches him on the arm and he pretends to act hurt.

"What? It's true." He motions toward me. "She admits she likes him and yet she refuses to go out with him. What's up with that?"

"My question exactly."

I close my eyes at the sound of Knox's voice. I want to slip under the table and disappear.

Slowly, I open one eye and peek out at him. "Please tell me you did not just hear that entire conversation."

He smiles and my stomach does that weird flippy thing when his eyes light up. "Only the really juicy parts."

I shake my head. I want to die. Or better yet, I want to strangle the two people sitting across from me.

"Can I get you guys something to drink?" he asks.

"Blue Moon," Colton says, nodding in that way guys do when they order beer.

"I'll take a shot of tequila and a Miller Lite."

I tap my toes under the table. Knox looks at me expectantly and I shake my head. "I'm not twenty-one."

"So?"

I narrow my eyes at him. "So I'm not old enough to drink."

Across the table, Jenna's shaking her head. "Just order something."

I look up at Knox and he seems to be waiting. I honestly don't even know what to do. I mean, it's not like I've never had a drink before, but never in an actual bar. Only at parties and stuff.

Knox studies me. "Do you always do everything by the rules?"

I laugh and nod. "Yes," I say. "Usually." And it's the truth. In some ways, I know it's my biggest flaw. Not exactly the following-the-rules part, but the do-what's-expected-of-me part. I hate to get in trouble or rock the boat. It's hard-wired into me or something.

He leans toward me, his breath warm against my cheek. "Isn't there some rule of logic, then, that says if you're attracted to me and you want to spend time with me, then you should just do it? Or am I wrong about the way we feel about each other?"

He pulls away slowly, our faces so close, I'm taken back to the memory of that kiss. No, he's definitely not wrong about the way I feel.

My heart beats so hard, I can feel it in my throat and in my ears. It's such a leap of faith to move forward with him. I know my life is a total mess, but I want him.

"Does that mean you're asking me out again?" I ask, sounding a hell of a lot more confident than I feel.

His lips don't move, but he's smiling. His eyes are shiny. "Does that mean you're saying yes?"

I bite my lip, then take the leap. "Yes."

CHAPTER 25

"I can't believe I actually agreed to this," I say to Knox as I hop into his truck. "You do realize that Joey hates me, right?"

He closes my door, then walks around and gets in. "She doesn't hate you."

"You weren't here in high school with us," I remind him. "The girl used to shoot daggers at me all through homeroom. She approached me in the girl's bathroom senior year just to tell me how glad she was that I was going away to school and that she hoped she never had to see my face again."

Knox tries to hide behind his hand, but it's obvious he's laughing.

"She really said that?"

"I swear on my life she did."

"Wow, what in the world did you do to piss her off?"

"I have no idea," I say, but that's not entirely true. Joey's always hated the rich girls. Once we were old enough to know we were different, she resented me for it.

"Well, she knows all about you and me," he says. "And she knows you're coming today."

"Are you saying she didn't try to warn you about me?" I pry.

He shrugs and I nod. I knew it.

"What did she say?"

"She told me you and Preston Wright had a thing back in the day," he says. "And that she doesn't think you're really the type to lower yourself for a guy like me."

The words hurt me. Lower myself? Do people think I act like I'm better than them? Is that who I used to be?

"She's talking about my past," I say. "It's been a long time since high school."

"Not that long," he says. "Two years."

"It might as well be a lifetime."

He doesn't argue with that.

I stick my hand out the window and let it ride the wind, remembering when I used to do this as a child. I glance over and see he's watching me from the corner of his eye.

I pull my hand back in, and scoot up next to him. He puts his arm around me and we ride like this the rest of the way to the lake.

We park and walk around to the lake side. There's a fire burning inside a ring of cement blocks. A little ways out from there, a large table has been set up with four chairs. Joey is busy spreading a navy tablecloth across the top. She turns as we walk up and I see her eyes dart to our linked hands.

Her eyebrows cinch together in the middle for a brief moment, then she forces a smile.

Nerves knot in my stomach. The look on her face confirms what I already suspected—Joey does not want her cousin dating me. I'm beginning to think this was not such a good idea for our first official date.

"Hey Joey," I say in the interest of making peace. "It's been a while."

She nods slowly. "Yes it has," she says. "When Knox told me he'd saved you from disaster that night, I thought surely he had to be talking about someone else. I thought you'd written us all off in Fairhope, never to return."

I'm not sure how to respond to that, but thankfully I don't have to.

"Leigh Anne." A tall, broad-shouldered man with wild brown hair steps around the corner of the house, then takes long strides toward us, his hand outstretched. There's a big smile across his face. "I'm sure we've crossed paths before when you and Joey were in school, but I'm not sure we ever officially met. I'm Rob, but you can just call me Uncle Rob."

He winks and shakes my hand, then claps Knox on the shoulder.

"It's really nice to meet you," I say. His smile is infectious and makes me feel a little better about the evening.

"What can we do to help?" Knox asks.

Joey pulls a bag from the back of her SUV. "You can take these and set them out on the table. We're almost ready with the food. I just need to pull the chicken off the grill."

Knox takes the large bag and we begin taking out plates, napkins and utensils and setting them around the table.

There is a cooler full of fresh fruit, cole slaw and some kind of homemade drinks bottled without labels. I pull all these from the back of the van and start setting them out on the table just as Joey brings over a plate of steaming chicken and veggie kabobs.

Everything smells so delicious, as if we're at a fancy restaurant instead of out on the lake in the middle of the woods.

"This looks amazing," I say as we all take our places behind one of the folding chairs.

Joey studies my face, searching for sarcasm, but I am being completely genuine. "Thanks," she says. Maybe her expression softens a bit.

"Let's say grace," Uncle Rob says. He grabs Joey's hand, then reaches across the space for mine.

I'm not used to praying before meals, but I can tell right away this is a tradition in their family. They do it almost without thinking. I take Rob's hand and then reach for Knox's. Once the circle is complete, Knox lowers his head and begins to speak.

"Dear heavenly father, we thank you for this mild weather and for the opportunity to come together here in this beautiful place," he says.

Everyone else has their eyes closed, but mine are open slightly, watching him. I never realized he was a religious kind of guy and it seems like a new layer of him is being unraveled in front of me.

"We thank you for the delicious food Joey has prepared for us and we also thank you for bringing Leigh Anne home to Fairhope and into our lives."

He squeezes my hand and my heart dances.

"We ask that you bless this food in your son's name. Amen."

"Amen."

We release hands and everyone takes their seat at the table, reaching out for various plates of food and filling their own to the top with fruit, veggies, slaw, chicken, and slices of home-made bread.

I take a bite of the chicken. "This is so incredible," I say. "What kind of seasoning do you use?"

Joey smiles as she puts a napkin across her lap. "I'll never tell."

Knox laughs. "That's Joey's special seasoning mix," he says.

"She claims she'll take it to the grave with her before she'll tell anyone what's in it."

"Knox keeps threatening to hide a secret camera in the kitchen so he can steal her recipe," Rob jokes before putting a huge spoonful of slaw in his mouth.

"And I'll kill him if he ever tries it." Joey kicks him under the table and Knox laughs and kicks her back.

The three of them all laugh and cut up with each other all through dinner, and I love the sound. My family never laughs around the dinner table. Hell, we hardly even talk around the dinner table, anymore. Here, though, the conversation flows easily.

"So, Leigh Anne, Knox tells me you're working at Brantley's," Rob says. "How do you like it out there?"

I hold my hand over my mouth until I can finish chewing the piece of squash I'd just stuffed in my mouth. "I love it," I say. "I've already made some really good friends and the money's good."

"I bet," Rob says.

Joey snorts and everyone looks at her.

"Sorry," she says. "It's just that I can't imagine why someone like you cares about the fifty bucks a night you probably make working at Brantley's."

Knox's hand slides over my knee and he gives her the evil eye.

"What?" she asks, leaning forward. "Her parents have more money than they know what to do with."

"My parents' money isn't my money," I say.

She meets my eye. "Isn't it?"

"What do you mean?"

She shrugs and takes a sip from the bottle in front of her. "I mean, have they ever denied you anything you ever wanted? If you went home right now and told them you needed a thousand bucks for a new purse or something, would they really say no? Or would they hand over their credit card?"

Her words are a punch to my gut. "It's not about that," I say.

"What is it about then?" she asks.

I shrug and pick at the lump of slaw on my plate. I've never really given it this much thought, so it's hard to make a rational argument out of it. Besides, she's right about my parents. If I asked them for money, they would hand it over no problem for something like a purse or a new car even. But that doesn't mean my parents always support me or give me what I want. How can I possibly begin to explain that to someone like Joey, who decided what she thought about me a long time ago?

"It's about independence," I say finally. "It's about working hard for something for myself instead of being handed something that comes with a whole list of rules and expectations attached."

Once the words are out of my mouth, I realize it's the truth. I'd never put words to it like that, but it was an honest and real response that makes me feel suddenly open and exposed. Beside me, Knox is staring. I shift uncomfortably.

"You've changed a lot since high school," she says, leaning back against her chair. If I'm not mistaken, there's a new respect in her eyes. "It's like when I got my first catering job outside of the bar. Don't get me wrong, I was really happy to have my dad's support with the business when I was getting my start, but he was sort of obligated to help me out."

"The hell I was," he says. "If your cooking sucked, I would have never hired you to do any of those jobs."

Joey rolls her eyes and smacks her dad on the arm. "I'll take that as a compliment."

"You should. I wouldn't hire just anyone to serve food in my bar, trust me."

"Anyway, my point is that your parents are supposed to support you and believe in you," she says. "But sometimes I guess you don't really start to believe in yourself until you get that outside validation or whatever."

Our eyes meet over the table and for the first time since sixth grade, we're playing nice.

Under the table, Knox's hand finds mine and for the moment, I belong.

CHAPTER 26

Dinner's been over for a while and the fire is dying down when we all decide to finally get up and clear the table.

Knox and Rob work on putting out the fire while Joey and I box up the leftovers and throw all the trash into a big black trash bag.

She pulls the navy tablecloth off and I see the beauty of the wood underneath for the first time. I'm mesmerized by the pattern. It's obviously a custom table, handcrafted with great care. There are three different colors of wood used to create a kaleidoscope design. I run my hand along the smooth top.

"This table is gorgeous," I say. "I can't believe you guys are using this outside. It had to have cost a fortune."

Joey shakes her head. "This is nothing," she says.

I have to look up to see if she's messing with me. "Nothing? I've never seen anything like this before. It's extraordinary."

Joey glances up at Knox who walks up and wraps his arms around me.

"Do you mean that?" he asks. "You really think it's nice?"

I nod and study the pattern again. "I love it."

"You should show her," Joey says.

"Show me what?" I pull away slightly and turn to question him.

He smiles. "Come with me."

We walk across the yard to the big shed nestled in the woods beside the house. The building is crudely constructed with basic walls and a tin roof. The door is pretty beat up and when he takes me through it, I see that there's nothing more to the floor than a concrete slab.

But when he flips on the light, what I see takes my breath away.

Inside the shed is the most gorgeous furniture I've ever laid eyes on. I let go of his hand and walk in, eager to get a closer look.

There's a dresser with several different woods mixed together, creating a geometric pattern along the front. I run my hand across the top of another dining table made of some kind of dark red wood that's so rich and beautiful.

A table on the far wall has several boxes of varying sizes lined up and I cross to get a better look. Many of them are made with mixed woods and textures, fitted together in such unique ways and shapes.

"I've never seen anything like this before," I say, opening the top of one of the large boxes. I gasp at the intricate work that had to have gone into this. "Did you make all this?"

He moves up behind me and my heart races. I'm wearing shorts and he's so close now, the edge of his jeans brushes the back of my leg. I shiver, wanting to lean my body into his.

"What do you think?"

I lower the top of the box, then run my fingers over the wood of another. "They're beautiful."

He steps to the side and I immediately miss the warmth of him even though it's got to be ninety degrees in here.

He picks up one of the smaller boxes. "I've been playing with a few different designs and materials."

He hands me the small box and I study it in awe. He's put a jade inlay across the top and the box itself is made with both light colored wood and a very dark brown wood used in a rotating boxed pattern.

"This had to have taken hours." My finger finds a small flaw in the wood and I am glad to find it. It lets me know he's human. Real.

"I spend a lot of time out here thinking. I like to listen to music and experiment with new ways to put things together."

I'm amazed at the detail in all of this work. It's more than just furniture or woodwork. It's art.

"The ones over on this wall are my favorite," he says, taking my hand and leading me across the room to the back wall. "I like to spend my days off sometimes going to lumber yards around the state, looking for something different and unique. A few months back, I found this pile of discarded wood at a little place near Florida. It's pine, but some of the sap got trapped inside the wood. The guy at the lumber yard said it was useless, but I thought it was kind of unique and cool."

He pulls a sheet off a small table and my hand goes to my mouth. The wood is flat and smooth and he's put some kind of shiny lacquer over the top, but I see what he means about the sap. It's trapped deep inside the wood like an amber bubble. Almost like a jewel embedded by nature.

"This is gorgeous," I say. "And you made this?"

"I did."

I watch as he runs his hand lovingly over the surface of the wood. I can feel his love and his passion for this place and every piece in it.

There's a depth to this guy I wasn't expecting. There's so much more to him than anyone realizes. People in town think he's nothing more than a loser with a troubled past, but looking around at all this beauty, I see a side to him no one else gets to see.

And I wonder why he's trusting me with it.

"Where did you learn to do all this?"

He looks away and shakes his head.

"What?"

When he looks at me, I see fear in his eyes. I know that look. It's my look. A mix of shame and pain and betrayal. This is the flash of darkness I've seen in his eyes before.

"You can tell me if you want." I move closer to him and put my hand on his cheek. "We both have our secrets. Scars we're afraid to let anyone see. Whatever it is, I won't judge you.

I think about my own secret. About what happened the night of my date with Burke Redfield. Am I ready to talk to Knox about that? I'm scared what he'll think of me. I'm scared he won't believe me or it will make things awkward between us. But at the same time, I desperately want to connect with someone who will understand.

He might be the one.

He swallows and puts his hand on mine. He looks down, avoiding my gaze. "It's not easy for me to talk about," he says. He shakes his head.

"You don't have to if you aren't ready."

"I want to tell you," he says. "I really need to tell you, because I'm scared if I don't, someone else will."

My insides twist and I flinch. I don't mean for him to notice, but he does.

He takes a step back and my hand drops to my side. "Someone already has, right?" he says. He runs his hand through his hair. "Shit. So tell me, what's the story everyone tells about me around here?"

I close my eyes briefly and suck a breath in through my nose. I have to tell him the truth, but I don't want him to be angry. "I've heard a couple of different things," I say. "Mainly that you got in trouble up in Chicago for drugs and assault and ended up in jail for a few years before you came down here."

He nods and bites his lip. "That's not as outrageous as I expected."

"Is it true?"

"What do you think?" he asks.

"If I thought it was true, I probably wouldn't be here right now," I say. "And even if it is true, I know you're not like that."

He leans against a large metal saw that's set up on this side of the room. "Technically, it's all true," he says. "I went to a juvenile detention facility when I was fifteen years old on charges of assault and possession."

I stay very still, waiting to hear the rest of the story.

"The possession part was true. I was really messed up from having to go live with my dad," he says. "I got into the wrong crowd up there real fast and for me, drugs were a good escape from having to think about how much I missed my mom or how much of an asshole my dad was." He shakes his head, as if trying to shake off the bad memories. "I definitely got in my fair share of fights too, but the person they charged me with assaulting?" He meets my eyes. "I didn't do that."

"Who was it?"

He hangs his head low, and I am not sure he's going to continue. "I don't really want to talk about it," he says. "It doesn't really matter, anyway. The person told the truth a few years later and they let me go."

The room is quiet for a moment, and I don't know what to say. I know he hasn't given me the whole story, but I don't want to press him either. I want him to share when he's really ready to share it. And maybe we're just not there yet.

"So, how does all that lead to you making furniture?" I ask, bringing the conversation back to where it first started.

He looks up and smiles. "Juvie is where I learned to do all this," he says. "Most of us were technically still in high school while we were there, so they had us take regular classes every day. English, math, whatever. But there were trade classes too. They stuck me in wood shop. Turns out I had a knack for it."

"That's putting it lightly," I say, touching the edge of the table next to me.

"I always knew it was something my grandfather was good at, because my mom used to bring me here to Fairhope as a kid. We'd stay in this lake house and spend time with my grandparents. I knew he'd built this house with his own hands and that he'd done all the woodworking himself," he says. "But I never really thought it was something I could do until I got to juvie."

"When I got out, it just didn't feel right to go to college," he explains. "I wanted to get out on my own. Do my own thing for a while. I knew this old house had burned up years ago, so I thought why not? Uncle Rob needed help with the bar and had an extra room over the garage, so it worked out perfectly."

"I'm sorry you had to go through all that," I say.

"Don't be," he says, walking back toward me. "I'm actually kind of grateful for my time at juvie. I was lucky, really. They wanted to try me as an adult for the assault charges, but my father intervened and made sure I went to JDC instead of prison. I mean, it still sucked and the assault charges were bullshit anyway, but at the same time, I knew I was on a bad path with those guys I thought were my friends at the time. And I was actually really glad to get away from my dad at the time. At least in juvie, I was able to stop doing drugs and find something that gave me purpose for the first time in my life."

He moves to stand next to the table with the exposed sap. He runs his finger along the upraised part where the sap is trapped inside.

"When my mom died, I was so lost," he says. There's a faraway look in his eyes and maybe some hidden tears. "I didn't even know my dad at all. I didn't remember him from when I was little and he never so much as sent me a card for my birthday or anything. When I got shipped off to him and taken away from everyone and everything I'd ever known and loved, I was angry. Broken. Maybe if he had welcomed me into his life and his new family, things could have been different, but he didn't. He reminded me every single day that he never wanted me in the first place. He had managed to claw his way out of the deep south and build this perfect life for himself. Big-shot career, beautiful young wife, twin girls who were just babies when I moved in, a huge house in the suburbs. He spent more money in a month than my mom made in two years working her job teaching school.

"I guess I reminded him of the life he'd had before he made it big. He wanted nothing to do with me, so I made it my mission to fuck up as much as humanly possible just to get his attention."

I put my hand on his arm.

"Getting away from him was bittersweet," he says. "I missed my freedom. I was angry for a very long time. But I found that I could really be myself when I was working with wood. I know it sounds weird, but it's true. I was desperate for some kind of outlet back then. Something that could give me the focus I needed. Something to pull me out of my own head and stop being so mad all the time.

"Once I got the basics down, I started to experiment. Different woods have different levels of strength, different colors that can be brought out in different ways. I had a good teacher who really went out of his way to mentor me in there. When I finally got out, this was all I really wanted to do."

I stare at him in awe, imagining the strength it must have taken to endure all that and still come out searching for something better in life.

"You're not like any guy I've ever met before," I say. I move to him, putting a hand on his chest so I know he hears me.

He runs a hand through his dark hair. "So you don't care that I'm a convicted criminal?"

"It doesn't change who you are," I say. "Or how I feel about you."

He twists his lips. "I doubt your parents would like it."

I laugh and lean back against the table. "My parents would go apeshit," I say. "You're definitely not what they have in mind for their little girl."

He swallows and his shoulders tense. "Where does that leave us?"

I shake my head. There's no easy answer to that question. "It leaves us right where we are, I guess. I can't live my whole life according to what my parents want," I say. It's the first time I've ever said anything like that out loud, but I realize it's something that's been on my mind since I first got home to Fairhope. When I was little, I always believed that what my parents wanted had to be what was best for me. Now, after all that's happened, I'm not so sure.

"So, you don't think I'm a loser for spending all my time working in here instead of going to college?"

I study him. "Is that something you're really worried about? That I'll think you're a loser for not going to school?"

He shrugs. "I know it's the right choice for me, but I also know it's something that's important to your family," he says. "I'm never going to be able to compete with guys like Preston Wright, or whoever, up at your fancy school in Boston. But that's not me." He looks around at the furniture he's created. "This is me."

"You're not anything like all those other guys. It's what I like best about you." I search his eyes so he knows I'm being sincere. "And all this? It's amazing. You're an artist."

Our eyes lock together and something passes between us. An energy I can't explain.

He steps toward me and hooks his fingers in the belt loops of my shorts.

I swallow, my heart pounding in my ears and my throat suddenly dry. My lips part slightly as he pulls me closer.

"I think you're amazing," he says, his voice low and so sexy it melts my insides.

He's biting that lower lip again and I can't take my eyes off of him.

Warmth shoots through my veins as his thumb brushes the bare skin just above my waistband. My whole body responds to his touch. And I want more.

His hands grip my waist and he lifts me off the ground, setting me on top of the table. My legs part and he steps into me. My hands go to his neck and I pull him in, our lips saying what our voices can't.

I wrap my legs around his waist and feel him press hard against me. A fire ignites everywhere his body touches mine.

Our kiss deepens and I can't get enough. I open; hungry for the taste of his tongue.

His hand slips under my shirt in the back and he presses his palm flat against the bare skin of my back, pulling me so close, not even air will fit between our bodies. We're tangled up in each other, and I never want to let go.

A moan escapes from me as his mouth travels across my jaw and down my neck. I lean my head back and close my eyes, passion boiling on the surface of my skin. I run a hand through his hair and his lips leave a trail of soft kisses across my neck and up toward my ear.

We're both out of breath, our bodies yearning for more, when he pulls away to look deep into my eyes.

"I've never been able to talk to anyone about these kinds of things," he says. "I'm not proud of my past, but it's a part of who I am. I'm still working through a lot of shit, but for some reason, I'm less broken when I'm with you."

"Maybe it's because we're both broken," I say.

He hugs me again and we hold each other until the thundering of our hearts begins to slow.

CHAPTER 27

Over the next few weeks, Knox and I are inseparable except when we're working.

Most evenings, he comes by Brantley's and sits with Colton at the bar before heading in to his shift at his uncle's bar. I usually get off work before he does and lately I've been hanging out at the bar a few nights a week. My mother doesn't ask where I am, but every word out of her mouth to me is toxic and tense. I avoid her at all costs.

Knox and I spend our afternoons and our days off out at the lake house. He is teaching me to use the saw and planer, but mostly, I just watch him work. I've also been spending some time inside the house, sweeping away any old debris, cleaning up anything that's too burned to save. Sometimes I bring a journal to write in. Knox says keeping a journal in jail helped him work through some of his anger and hurt, so I am trying my hand at getting my feelings down on paper.

It's funny how it's hard to be honest, even with myself.

He still hasn't asked me to tell him what happened up at school, and I haven't brought it up. The closer I get to him, the more I realize I'll eventually have to tell him. But for now, I'm just not ready.

Every once in a while, I'll see Molly's face in a magazine or news report, but I think the media is getting tired of her story. According to Sophy, the case should go to trial early next year and once that's over, one way or another, things will begin to calm down.

I've gone out with my friends a few times and Penny asks me to lunch a couple times a week, but more and more I'm saying no. I tell them I have to work or that I have plans. As hard as I try to recapture the depth of our old friendship when we're together, it all feels very superficial. I know Penny thinks I'm being weird for not hanging out and partying with them every night, but the more time I spend with Knox, the less I want to be with anyone else.

"The thing is, I'm just not the same girl I used to be," I say to him one night as we sit on the dock looking up at the stars. "I don't fit in with those girls anymore. Still, I know they're pissed at me for being home and not hanging out with them."

"You don't have to be anyone you're not," he says. He picks up my hand and lays a soft kiss on my knuckles. "You don't owe anyone anything."

"But they were my best friends, you know? I feel guilty for not spending more time with them."

"Why?" He lies back against the dock, his hands behind him like a pillow. "People are coming in and out of our lives all the time. Just because someone was your friend two years ago doesn't mean you're still going to have the same things in common now. Especially when your life experiences are so different."

I'm falling for him. Hard. I can feel it so deep down in my heart, but it terrifies me. Am I really capable of loving someone? Am I really worthy of being loved back?

I can't face those questions. Not yet.

"What about you?" I ask, lying down next to him. I nestle in to the crook of his arm and place my arm across his chest. "Do you still talk to any of your old friends in Chicago?"

He shakes his head and gets that faraway look in his eyes he sometimes gets when he talks about his past. "I didn't really ever have any true friends in Chicago."

"No friends in Chicago. No friends here in Fairhope except your cousin and me. How is that possible?"

"What do you mean?"

"I mean, you're the sweetest, most creative man I've ever known in my life. You're easy to talk to. You're kind. Funny. I would think a guy like you would have swarms of friends," I say.

He turns his head a little toward me and our lips are almost touching. He answers in a near-whisper. "No one but you sees all that in me."

"Only because you don't show them the real you," I say.

"Not everyone in the world is willing to overlook my past, the way you are."

I lean in and press my lips to his. "Then everyone else in the world is missing out."

CHAPTER 28

The next day, we are working on a new idea Knox has for a wood and leather chair when he realizes he's out of upholstery nails.

"I need to run into town to get more," he says. "Want to come with me?"

I shrug. "Sure."

He smiles and takes my hand, leading me to the truck.

The wind is blowing hard today and some of the sweltering heat has lifted. As we drive toward town, I point out the dark clouds overhead. By the time we reach the hardware store, the rain is pouring down so hard we can hardly see five feet in front of us.

I'm wearing flip-flops, shorts and a tank top. I'm going to be soaked through. Knox rummages through the space behind the seat and pulls out a tattered green rain coat.

He holds it over his head and runs over to my side of the truck, doing his best to cover me up as we make a dash toward the front of the hardware store. There are a couple of major holes in the old coat, though, and by the time we get inside, we're both drenched anyway. I grab the coat and put my finger through one of the holes.

"Nice umbrella," I tease.

He grabs my finger and kisses the tip.

I can't stop laughing. I go up on my toes and kiss him, our hands clasped.

"Leigh Anne?"

My body tenses at the sound of my mother's voice. I pull away from Knox, suddenly freezing cold from the rain soaking my clothes. I let go of his hand.

My whole life, I've never known my mother to purposely go to the fucking hardware store. Ever.

"Mom?" I wipe the rain from my forehead and push my hair back. I take a step away from Knox, then immediately hate myself for it. "What are you doing here?"

Her lips press into a straight line and she looks from me to Knox and back. "I could ask you the same thing."

"We were just coming to get some nails," I say, but I know that's not what she is really asking me.

Mom stares at him for a long moment, before finally making that condescending clicky sound she makes with her tongue. I hate that sound. "Aren't you going to introduce me to your friend?"

"Oh." I squirm in my soaked flip-flops, not sure what game she's playing. "This is Knox Warner, Mom. Remember? You met him the night I first came home. He got me home safe after my accident."

"It sure is," Mom says; her smile tense and fake. She holds her hand out to him. "I guess it completely slipped my mind."

Beside me, Knox shifts his weight before finally taking my mother's hand. I can feel the tension radiating off of him. From the corner of my eye, I can see that he keeps looking at me, and

I have no idea what he expects me to do. Kiss him right here in front of my mom just to prove a point?

My mother looks at him again, her face full of doubt and judgment. "Well, I've got to get going," she says. "I only stopped in here to pick up a new hammer and picture hanging kit for the church. We're hanging up the new portrait of the pastor this afternoon before the dedication of the new social hall."

I nod and smile, but just want this moment to be over already.

"You'll be home for dinner tonight?" she says, eyebrows raised.

"I have to work tonight," I say.

She narrows her eyes and nods. "Right."

She glances from Knox to me, as if suggesting I'm lying about work just to be with him. She lets out a tedious sigh before sailing past us and out into the rain.

I turn and watch as she lifts her umbrella and walks away, each step careful and deliberate.

Anger flows through my veins, mingled with disappointment. Why did I let go of his hand?

I need to apologize, but I can't even find the words. We stand there near the entrance, and I can't meet his eyes. The carefree mood we had is long gone.

Finally, he breaks the silence for me. "What exactly just happened here, anyway?"

I look up and see the anger on his face. "I'm sorry," I say. "My relationship with my mother is complicated."

"And what about your relationship with me?" he asks. "Does that mean anything to you?"

"Don't do that." I reach out to him; put my hand on his arm.

"Don't do what? Don't be honest with you about how I feel?" He pulls away from my touch. "I don't like to be treated like I'm not even standing here. I don't ever want to feel like I'm an embarrassment. My father used to do that shit to me all the time. When I moved to Chicago, he would parade his new family around like they were royalty, but me? He refused to even acknowledge me as his son. Do you have any idea how hurtful that is? I'm not going to be treated like that, Leigh Anne. Not by you or anyone."

"What is it you expect of me, then? You want me to run after her? And tell her what? That I've kissed you? That I like you and want to spend time with you? What do you want me to do?"

He runs his hand through his hair. "I just want you to be real with me," he says. "I've opened myself up to you in a way I haven't with any other girl. And that girl? The one I've been talking to and spending all this time with every day for weeks? I'm falling in love with her. Only, the problem is, the second you get together with your old friends or see your mother, you become someone else. Someone I'm honestly not sure I like very much."

I step toward him, but he shakes his head and raises his hands as he backs away.

He walks off toward the back of the store and I stand there near the entrance, powerless to even move.

CHAPTER 29

I don't go to the bar after my shift at the restaurant tonight.

It's late and I'm exhausted. For a short, perfect few weeks, Knox and I were able to exist in our own little bubble. Boston felt far away and I was settling in to a comfortable place.

I knew it couldn't last, but I had hoped it wouldn't end so soon.

Seeing my mother today at the hardware store brought the curtain down on the carefree mood of these few weeks.

Now, I'm not sure what to do. If I keep seeing Knox, my mother will never let me hear the end of it. She'll make my life hell and she'll never accept him into our home the way Knox's family accepts me. I know I won't be able to change her mind. He's simply not the kind of guy she wants me to be with and she's far too judgmental to see past his circumstances. Even if she could find a way to deal with the whole bartender thing, there's no way she'll ever forgive the jail thing.

I want to stand up to her, but the thought of the endless

arguments makes me feel tired deep in my bones. I had to be strong in Boston on a daily basis, but part of the reason I came home in the first place was because I got so tired. I started to lose my sanity, I think. Toward the end of this past semester, I was in a very dark place.

If I am in a constant fight with my mother, I know it will take me back to that place.

But at the same time, losing Knox will devastate me.

He understands me. When I'm with him, I can drown out the rest of the noise in my head and actually laugh without forcing it. I can't lose him.

The war going on in my brain won't stop, so I drive home and am careful not to make any noise as I come in. It's already after eleven, so my parents should be sleeping. All I want to do is go up to my room and crawl into bed. I'm tempted to search the hall bathroom for some of my mother's sleeping pills so I won't end up lying in bed with my mind spinning in circles for hours. I avoid the creaking stair three from the top and open the door to my room.

Before I disappear inside, though, my mother says my name.

I want to cry. I want to yell at her to go away and leave me alone. But I keep telling her I'm not a child, so it's probably not a good idea to act like one.

I square my shoulders and turn to face her.

She's in her bathrobe and matching nightgown. Even her slippers match.

"I wasn't expecting you home until later," she says. "You've been staying out so much lately."

I nod, bracing myself for the insult that's coming.

She clutches her hands in front of her body. "Is that who you've been spending all this time with? This Knox boy?"

"Yes." I keep my answers short and simple, not giving her

extra ammunition for whatever it is she's been waiting up to say to me.

She puts her hand on the banister and takes a few steps toward me. "Listen, I know, over the past couple of years, you've been through more than anyone your age should have to go through," she begins. "I know it was your dream to go to school up there and it has to be difficult to be home now, with your future up in the air. I get it."

I lean against the door frame and stare at my shoes. I have braced for an argument. I have no idea how to respond to compassion. I don't trust it.

"It's only natural for you to come home and feel restless," she says. "I feel like your father and I have done our best to stay out of your way while you explored some new choices. You wanted to get a job, fine. Of course, you know you don't need to work as long as you're going to school and still under our roof, but I can understand your need to do your own thing for a while."

I take deep breaths, counting in and out, like my counselor back in Boston taught me. Still, my toe taps wildly inside my boot.

"Now, whatever phase it is you're going through, I wish you'd let us help instead of turning to destructive behavior."

There it is. The dig she's been leading up to. And she isn't finished. My hand curls into a fist and my fingernails dig into my palm.

"I assumed you were spending some time with this boy," she says. "I'm not stupid. I've seen him pick you up here a few times in that disgusting truck of his. What I did not realize, however, is just how far out of hand things had become."

For the first time since she started this little speech, I actually look at her face. Her expression is all compassion, but I know my mother is good at wearing masks. She doesn't have a truly compassionate or empathetic bone in her body.

"When I saw the two of you together today in that store?" Her hand goes to her heart and she closes her eyes, as if she's physically in pain. "Oh, Leigh Anne. I realized how twisted this whole mess has gotten you. You're just not seeing clearly. You're not making good decisions. The way you looked at each other? I feel I have to step in—"

"Like you stepped in with Burke?" His name hasn't passed my lips in a very long time and the bitterness in my voice surprises even me.

"Now, you know your father and I did everything we could in that situation," she says, putting her hand up as if telling me to stop.

The fact that she uses the word situation to describe what happened to me proves she has no true understanding for what I'm going through. She cares more about her plans for me than she actually does about me. I've always known it, but tonight it stings more than ever.

Why do I continue to sacrifice myself to please her?

"You know that you never once asked me what I wanted while we were there?" I say. I wasn't planning to talk about this tonight, but it spills out of me, and once I've started, I can't stop. "We sat in the dean's office and not once did you talk to me about what I wanted or what I needed."

"Of course we did," she says, her face wrinkling. "All we thought about the whole time we were there was what was best for you, sweetheart."

"That's not the same thing. Why can't you see that?" I shout. My chest tightens and my breath becomes shallow. "My whole life, it's always been about what you want for me. What you think is best for me. It's never once been about what I want or feel or what I need."

She lifts her chin. "I can't believe you would say such a thing. If we hadn't been there to protect you, just think what might have happened," she says. She slices a pointed finger through the air. "Look at this poor girl, this Molly person. She's being raked over the coals every single day, her face splattered all over the news every night. Is that what you wanted?"

"No, of course not, but that doesn't mean I wanted him to get away with it, either," I say. "That doesn't mean I wanted to have to keep my mouth shut about it for the rest of my life, pretending nothing happened. Hiding from it, like it was my fault, somehow."

"I never said it was your fault," she says, lowering her voice. There are tears in her eyes, as if it's me who has hurt her instead of the other way around. "But we had to do what was best for you and for our family. A long, drawn-out hearing or trial, even if we had somehow been able to keep it out of the press—which there's really no way we could have—would have drained us all, and for what? The small chance that they would believe you?"

Her words cut through me like knives. And the worst part of it is that she thinks she's being supportive. She's only thinking of herself in this whole thing.

"I guess we'll never know," I say, tears stinging my eyes.

I can't stay here. I can't live like this anymore.

I turn and grab my overnight bag from the corner of my bedroom. I rip open the dresser drawers and start throwing in tank tops and underwear, a pair of jeans, some shorts. I'm still wearing my work pants and shoes. My mind races. I want to gather what I can and get the fuck out of this place. I'm suffocating here.

"Leigh Anne, what in the world do you think you're doing?"

"I'm leaving," I say as I breeze past her into my bathroom. I toss my toothbrush and makeup into a plastic bag sitting on the counter and throw it into the overnight bag. I zip it up and throw it over my shoulder.

She blocks the doorway. "You're not going anywhere angry like this, do you hear me?"

During this whole conversation, I've barely even looked at her face, but now I look straight into her eyes. I make sure she sees me. Hears me.

"I hear you," I say. "I just don't care what you have to say anymore. Now, please, get out of my way."

She flinches. "I will not," she says. "If you walk out of this house—"

"What? You'll take away my credit cards? I don't care about any of that. I have my own money now, remember?"

She pushes air from her lips and jerks her head. "You can't have more than a couple hundred dollars, Leigh Anne. How long do you think that will really last?"

"I have over a thousand dollars saved up from working at Brantley's," I say. "And I can always pick up more shifts if I need to."

Her confidence falters and she crosses her arms in front of her chest. "Leigh Anne, you don't have to go anywhere," she says. "I know you're angry, but we can work this out, honey."

I shake my head. "What you really mean is, eventually I'll do what I always do, right? I'll be a good girl and do exactly what you tell me to do, because I don't have a mind of my own. Well, I'm not going to be that person anymore," I say. "I'm so tired of sacrificing who I am and what I want to be just to please you."

I push past her and practically run down the stairs. She follows me, calling my name, but I don't stop. I don't even turn around once.

I let the screen door in the back slam behind me as I get into my car and drive away.

CHAPTER 30

Rain pelts my windshield as I drive away from my parents' house.

Tears of anger and frustration stream down my face and my breath comes in hiccups and choked sobs. I pull off the road about a mile away and let the sorrow spill out of me. I've had several breakdowns since that night, but this is the worst. All my walls are tumbling down. Everything I believed about my own life and about myself has been shattered.

I have wasted years feeling responsible for my mother's happiness.

I can blame her all I want, but it's my fault, too. I've allowed her to make choices for me. She may not ask me what I want, but when have I ever once spoken up? The only thing I ever did on my own was say goodbye to Fairhope so I could make a new life for myself. I was so proud of myself back then. The look on my mother's face when I told her I'd broken things off with Preston and was taking that scholarship was priceless. It wasn't that I wanted to hurt her, but rather that I wanted to be my own person for once. I wanted to see what life was like without her voice in my ear.

But Burke Redfield took all of that away from me. He stole everything from me.

And instead of standing up for me, my parents helped him cover it up.

The truth of it hits me in the chest and I collapse against the steering wheel. I've held this in too long. It's too much to carry by myself. If I don't talk about this, if I don't tell someone, I'm going to fall apart.

Knox is right. I haven't allowed myself to open up, even though he was brave enough to open up to me. I have kept these walls up because my parents asked me to. They told me it would be the best thing for me.

But they were wrong.

I lift my head and take a few ragged breaths, then turn the car around and head to Rob's bar, praying it's not too late.

CHAPTER 31

The parking lot is empty. I pull all the way around the bar to make sure he didn't park out back, but there's no sign of his truck.

I beat my hand against the steering wheel. I have no idea if he's at his uncle's or if he's gone out to the lake tonight to work.

I need to see him.

I pull my phone out of my bag to text him and ask him to meet me, but headlights flash in my rearview mirror and I look up. Through the rain, I can just make out Knox's truck as he parks beside me and gets out.

I throw my phone onto the passenger side and get out of the car, not even caring that it's pouring rain.

We meet in front of his truck, our bodies illuminated by the headlights. I throw my arms around him and press my face into his chest.

"I'm so sorry," I say over the sound of the storm. "I never meant to hurt you."

"Your hands are shaking," he shouts. He takes my face in his hands and lifts my head up. "What happened? Are you okay?"

"I don't know anymore," I say. Inside, my heart is pounding. Everything else is spiraling out of control in my life and all I want to do is hold on to him.

"I'm so sorry for how I acted earlier," he says. "I completely overreacted. I was coming to talk to you when I saw your car speed past me. I followed you back here," he says. "I needed to see you. I wanted to apologize for what happened today."

I shiver as the rain pours down on us. I press closer to him, gathering his shirt in my fist. "No, you were right, Knox. I'm so fucked up when it comes to my mom. I've spent my whole life worried what she'll think of me. Of my choices," I say, raising my voice as the storm intensifies around us.

"It's okay," he says.

"No, it's not okay." Tears are coming so hard now, I just let them fall. I can't hold them back anymore. "I'm not okay. I'm a complete mess and you deserve more than that."

Knox wraps his arms around me. He presses his mouth close to my ear. "What I said earlier, in the hardware store? About falling in love? I wasn't being completely honest with you."

My heart sinks and I pull away, my eyes searching his.

"I'm not falling," he says. "I'm already there. Head over heels, helplessly in love with you. And no matter what it is you're holding back, I'll wait for you. I swear to god, I'll do whatever it takes. Whatever you want. I just don't want to lose you."

As he says it, I understand what he's been telling me. He's right. I haven't completely let him in, and he knew it before I did. I want nothing more than to say I love him too. But I can't.

I haven't allowed myself to love.

Standing here in the rain, I know this is it. This is the moment I either trust him with the truth or I walk away. I can't protect my heart and give it to him at the same time.

Fear rushes through me. I'm scared to death, but I want this. I want him.

"I have to tell you," I start.

I open my mouth to speak again, but a sob escapes and I have to lift my hand to cover my mouth.

Knox lifts me up in his arms and presses my shivering body tight to his own. He carries me through the rain to the back door of the bar. He somehow manages to get his key in the lock and pull me into the darkness.

The door closes, shutting the rain out and it's like we're in a cocoon, sheltered from the noise and the rest of the world. He flips on the lights and I see that we're in a storage room piled with boxes.

He sets me down. With a soft touch, he wipes the rain from my forehead, then runs the back of his knuckles gently across my cheek and under my eyes. "I don't want to rush you into anything," he says. "I love you, Leigh Anne. The last thing in the world I want to do is cause you pain."

I shake my head, the tears still fresh. "I need to do this," I say. "You're right. I've been holding back, too scared that if I tell you the truth, I'll get hurt. But I don't want to shut you out. I need to talk about this."

Sobs threaten my voice again and I try to take a breath.

He takes my hand. "Here, follow me," he says. "I'll make us a couple of drinks and see if I can find some towels or blankets around here somewhere. We don't have to rush this, okay? You can take all the time you need."

He leads me into the bar and just as he flips the switch to turn on the lights, lightning crashes somewhere way too close and the whole room plunges back into darkness.

We freeze, waiting, but the power doesn't come back on. It's silent in here except for the sound of the rain on the roof and the rumbling of thunder.

"Wait right here," Knox says.

"Where are you going?" I ask as he lets go of my hand.

"I've got some matches behind the bar, and I'm pretty sure I can find a few candles if I look around," he says. A few seconds later, he lights a match and the space around him glows with a golden light.

He smiles at me, then sucks in a breath and drops the match to the floor. He laughs and lights another.

I can't help but smile at him despite the pain in my heart. He tosses a book of matches at me and I catch them.

"Just in case," he says.

He shakes out the match in his hand and lights a third. He searches through some cabinets for a moment and finally pulls out two white pillar candles. He lights them both, sets one on the bar and carries the other with him into the back room.

Instead of sitting down on a bar stool, I hop up on top of one of the nearby tables and wait.

Knox comes back a few minutes later with a couple of blankets. He wraps one around my shoulders and pulls me in for a kiss.

"If you're not ready, I'll wait," he says again.

"I want to tell you. If you're still willing to listen."

"Of course," he says. He sets the candle down on the table and uses the chair as stepping stool. We both sit together on the table top, the light of the candles flickering around us.

My heart is racing and my skin feels heavy. My hands tremble as I pull the blanket tighter around my shoulders.

Knox waits patiently as I take several deep breaths in and out, making sure my voice is strong and my heart is calm.

When I'm finally ready, I push aside all my doubts and fears, and I start from the beginning.

CHAPTER 32

"When I left Fairhope after high school, I was on top of the world," I start. "I had spent my whole life doing what everyone else wanted me to do, even down to dating Preston Wright. But what my parents didn't know—well, what no one really knew—was that Preston had cheated on me several times. The day before Valentine's Day, my senior year, I walked in on him with one of my best friends. Bailey Houston. Do you know her?"

Knox shakes his head.

"It really broke my heart. Until then, I had planned on sticking around here in Fairhope like my parents wanted instead of taking the scholarship up north."

"Wait, your parents didn't want you to go to school in Boston? Why not?

I sniff and wipe at my runny nose with a laugh. "Because my mother had her heart set on me marrying Preston Wright."

Knox reaches in his pocket and hands me a tissue.

"Thanks." I wipe my face and nose and keep going. "Anyway, I had planned to stay here and follow my mother's master plan.

I'd go to Fairhope Coastal U. Marry Preston. Be rich and respected as his wife. For a while, I thought that's what I wanted, too. But after he cheated on me with Bailey, I realized it was all a lie. This life I was living was a pretty picture on the outside, but it wasn't real. On the inside, it was hollow and meaningless and I realized that's not who I wanted to be for the rest of my life."

Knox is listening to every word, and I know I'm stalling, but in order to understand what that night meant to me—what it ruined for me—I had to start from the beginning.

"So after a lot of soul searching, I decided to break free. I decided to stop doing what my parents wanted and do something I wanted, for a change. For the first time in my whole life, I made a decision that was all about me and what I wanted for my future," I say. "To some people that might not sound like much, but to me, it was huge."

"I can see that," he says.

"When I got to school, I was probably more excited than I'd ever been in my life," I say. "Too excited to realize just how naive I was, I guess. Here in Fairhope, I was a big fish in a small pond, but there? There I was a very tiny fish in a very big ocean."

I think about my first day moving in to the dorm room and how, once my parents left, I felt somehow both incredibly small and big at the same time.

"The first semester was a whirlwind, really. I was having a ball, meeting lots of new people, struggling to keep up with my classes but still staying up half the night talking to the other girls in my dorm. Regular college stuff."

Knox waits patiently, not saying a word, but his eyes are glued to my face.

"I decided not to come home for Christmas break because it was such a long trip home," I say. "And to be honest, I just didn't want to spend the whole break listening to my mother's shit about how I'd made the wrong choice and how I'd screwed things up with Preston."

I think about that winter and tension knots up in my stomach. I feel another sob coming, but I choke it back. If I lose it now, I'll never get through this.

"I spent my break mostly catching up on my studies and exploring campus and Boston," I say. "I even took the train into New York a couple of times. It was the first time in my life I'd really traveled on my own."

I swallow down the lump in my throat.

"Well, one night when I was in New York City, I decided to walk over to Rockefeller Center to see the big tree. You know the one where the people ice skate and everything?" He nods. "I'd seen it on TV a million times, so I thought why not? So, there I am, staring up at this tree like a stupid tourist and this guy comes up beside me. He starts up a conversation and when I look over, I think I recognize him. Then, as he's talking, I realize wow, this guy is Burke Redfield."

"The actor?" He's confused at first, startled. Then he puts it together. He knows. I can see it as his face falls. I feel his body tense from head to toe. "He's the guy who has been all over the news."

I hold back another sob. "Yes," I say simply. I know I could probably end it there and let him draw his own conclusions, but I want to talk through this. I want him to be a witness to my story. "We got to talking and then we both realized that, hey, we go to the same school. I honestly don't know how I didn't know that before, but anyway, we ended up catching dinner together that night in the city, and exchanging phone numbers and email addresses. I was completely crushing on him at the time. I even called my mom to tell her about it.

"When we got back to campus for spring semester, I didn't

hear from him for a while, but it was like I saw him everywhere," I say. "We said 'hey' a couple of times, but I had pretty much given up hope on him ever really asking me out. Of course, I'd told all my friends about us meeting in New York and how I had this major crush on him, so everyone was so excited for me when he emailed me that March to ask if I wanted to go out to dinner and a movie. I said yes so fast! And must have spent something like five hours with all the girls on the floor of my dorm trying to find the perfect outfit for my date."

The tears begin to flow again as I think of that night and how excited I had been. I thought I was living some kind of fairytale.

Knox puts his hands on my leg as he waits for me to continue.

"He picked me up in this sporty car and took me to some fancy restaurant downtown," I say. "We were having a pretty good time, but the more we talked, the more I realized he was all about Burke. Whenever I tried to talk about myself or bring up anything about my past or my life, he always found a way to turn it around so he could talk about himself or his career. Still, it was Burke Redfield, you know? He was one of the most sought-after guys in the country and he had asked me out. I kept reminding myself how lucky I was to be there. How most girls would kill to listen to him talk about his career and all the actors he knows.

"After dinner, I thought he was going to take me to a movie, but as he drove, I realized he was taking us out of town." My voice cracks a little bit and my chest tightens. "I didn't say anything at first, but after a little while of driving out in the middle of nowhere, I finally asked him where in the world we were going, stupidly thinking that maybe he knew about some exclusive theater in a nearby town or something."

I laugh at my own stupidity, but it comes out as more of a cry. Knox squeezes my leg.

"He just kept telling me I'd see, like he was taking me to some exclusive, ultra-cool place that would blow my mind." I pause and take a couple of deep breaths. "But when he pulled off onto some weird dirt road and parked, I knew something was definitely wrong. I tried to laugh it off and just go with it. I mean, for all I knew, this was normal college behavior. He said he'd just brought me here so we could have some privacy. He gave me this line about how he hated always being in the spotlight and never being able to really be alone with anyone. He told me he thought I was really special and that he just wanted to kiss me without the paparazzi sticking a camera in my face."

I can't control the tears now and I just let them fall. They fall onto Knox's hand, but he doesn't move. He just holds tight to me as my body trembles.

"At first, I kissed him back. I kind of liked him and thought we were just having a good time. Other than being conceited, he hadn't done anything that set off warning signals, but in the back of my mind, I think I knew something was off. At the same time, I had no idea what I could really do about it. We were out in the middle of fucking nowhere, you know? What was I going to do? Get out and try to walk home? Hitchhike? We hadn't seen a car in ages. I wasn't even sure I would know which direction to go if I tried to walk.

"So, I figured it was better not to rock the boat. I thought I could handle it. I let him kiss me for a minute. It started out nice. I mean, it wasn't like he was the first guy I'd made out with or anything. But then he started to take it too far. He kissed me harder and started to move his hand higher up on my thigh."

I squirm, not wanting to think about that night or how he'd

made me feel. But I need to. I have to talk about this. I've kept quiet for way too long.

"I tried to pull away, but there wasn't exactly a lot of room to move away inside that tiny little sports car. I laughed it off and told him that I'd had a really great time, but that it was getting kind of late and I had something I needed to do in the morning."

Knox's hands tighten into fists and his breathing has become shallow.

"He backed off for a minute, but he didn't make any move to start the car or take me home. He started kissing me again and this time he got pretty aggressive. When I told him I wanted him to take me back, he got really angry. It was like some switch inside him got flipped. He started yelling at me, saying that I'd had no problem spending all his money at dinner, but now that he wanted just a little something from me, I wasn't willing to return the favor."

I flinch at the memory.

"He grabbed me and pulled me across the stick shift toward his side of the car and I panicked. I reached for the door and pushed it open, but when I tried to get out he grabbed the back of my dress and pulled me, really hard, back into the car. My head smacked against the door frame and started gushing blood."

My fingers trace the smooth upraised scar just above my temple.

"I started to feel light-headed, but I knew I had to get out of there. I wasn't thinking clearly and just ripped out of his grasp and started running. The strap on my dress was ripped and I just remember that I kept trying to put it back in place, but it kept falling as I ran."

I hang my head low and take a moment to steady myself, the memories flooding through me, threatening to wash me overboard. I struggle to breathe through the tears and Knox moves to sit next to me, putting his strong arms around me and pulling my head against his shoulder.

"You don't have to keep going if it's too hard," he whispers.

But I can't stop now. For the past year and a half, I haven't been allowed to talk about this. I haven't had anyone who was willing to listen and who could understand the pain of what I went through. I need to get it out. I need to know he can still love me even after he knows.

"No, I want to tell you," I say. I inhale and my breath hitches. "If there's any hope of a future between us, you need to know."

"I'm here," is all he says. And it's all I need to hear.

When I'm ready, I swipe the tears from my cheeks and sit up. My voice is oddly calm and I feel numb thinking of what happened next. I am able to recite it as if I were merely a spectator in the whole thing instead of someone who lived the horror of it all.

"I didn't get far before Burke caught up with me," I say. "He lifted me up like I was nothing. Like I was as light as a feather. I'll never forget that feeling of being weightless, helpless against his strength. He carried me back toward the car, but stopped short, then threw me on the ground just inside the tree line. For a split second, I thought he was going to kill me. He had this look in his eyes." I grimace and fresh tears sting the corners of my eyes. "He was excited. Full of power and control. He pinned me down on the ground, and the whole time he was doing it, all I could say was 'stop' over and over."

Rage tenses my muscles.

"You know what he said to me?" I shake my head, hearing his voice so clear in my mind. "He said, 'I wouldn't have to do this if you would have just let me fuck you.' As if it was my fault for not just giving in in the first place. As if it was my choice."

Knox's face is all straight lines and pure anger. "I swear to God, I'm going to kill him," he says and I see that his eyes are wide and filled with tears.

"When he was finished, he just got up and told me to get back in the car. I didn't know what else to do except just do as I was told. I got in the car with that mother fucker and sat next to him in silence the whole drive home. When I got out, he actually said goodnight and opened the door for me. As if nothing had happened. As if he was some kind of gentleman."

Knox caresses my hair. "I'm so sorry," he says. "Did you tell anyone?"

I close my eyes. "Not at first. It was really late and most people were already asleep. I got up to my room as fast as I could and stripped off my dress and threw it in the trash. I got in the shower and just sat in there for the longest time, turning the water hotter and hotter, then I crawled into bed and fell asleep. The next day, everyone was asking me about the date and gushing over how cute Burke is and how it must have been so amazing. I didn't know what to do. Part of me just wanted to pretend nothing happened. I thought that if I told everyone it was a fun night, then maybe I could make it true. I even started telling myself that really he didn't do anything wrong. It was my fault it turned out the way it did. If I had just—"

I choke back another sob. I have spent so long blaming myself for what happened, but actually saying it out loud, I hear how stupid it sounds.

"It wasn't your fault," he says. "Oh, Leigh Anne, please tell me you know that this wasn't your fault?"

"I know," I say. And I do. But it helps to hear someone agree with me. Believe me. "I tried to act like everything was okay, but my roommate Sophy knew something was up. She kept asking questions about what happened to my head and how come I didn't want to talk about my date. I finally told her and I guess saying it out loud made me see it for what it was.

"He raped me."

Even now, the words stumble against my tongue. It's such a nightmare; it doesn't seem possible that it really happened to me. I have spent so much time trying to reason it away. Trying to make sense of it all.

Only, it doesn't make sense. It will never make sense to me why someone so handsome and wealthy—a guy who could have anything and almost any girl he wanted—would force anyone to do what he did to me.

"When did you say this happened?" he asks. He's holding my hands now so tight, and the pressure feels good. He's holding on to me and anchoring me to this place. He's keeping me from disappearing into the nightmare memories of that night.

"March of last year," I say. "A few weeks before spring break, my freshman year."

Knox shakes his head. "You've lived with this secret for a year and a half?"

"It's not a secret from everyone," I tell him. "Sophy talked me into going to the school clinic and requesting a rape kit. I knew it had been a couple of days, but she said sometimes they can still gather some evidence. I had bruises and scrapes on my leg. The cut on my forehead. I even pulled my ripped dress out of the trash and gave it over to campus police. Everything snowballed from there, and I know this makes me sound awful, but as soon as the police and nurses and administrators got involved, I wished I had never told anyone."

"Why? What happened?"

I shake my head. "The whole process was awful. I had nurses examining me, making me get naked while they poked and prodded and gathered samples. They took pictures of me, completely humiliated me. The whole time, I felt like I had done something wrong. And when they asked me who..." I sigh and pick at the edge of my shirt. "Their eyes would go wide and they would excuse themselves and start whispering. It didn't take long for someone from the administration to step in. They told me I could demand a hearing at the school, where I could face him in person and accuse him and try to get him expelled from the school, but in the same breath, they told me that it would become a media circus. They said it would be in my best interest to keep the whole thing off the record. They promised to take care of me, but the truth is that they kept me completely in the dark.

"Every time I asked if there was anything I needed to do or where things were in the process, they would put me off, claiming they were still working it out or whatever. Finally, the dean of students called me into his office and told me that it had been decided that there wasn't enough evidence to warrant any kind of official hearing."

"They buried it."

I nod, not sure what he's going to think of me now that he knows. The few people who know have all treated me completely different after they found out. Conversations become awkward and their eyes fill with either pity or fear.

"What about your parents?" he asks. "If you tell them, maybe they can do something."

I shake my head and give a sad smile. "They were the ones who convinced me not to file an official report," I say. "They kept saying no one needed to involve the press and that it was in my best interest to just move on.

"But now this girl has come forward," I say. "Molly Johnson. She was a freshman this year and he raped her, too. Only she didn't keep quiet like I did. I don't know her, but I've seen her around campus. I had been doing the best I could to bury the memories and just try to survive and get through it, but when she came forward, everything came rushing back. All the anger and the hurt and the helplessness. I had a complete emotional breakdown and my parents said I couldn't stay there. As soon as the semester was over, I came home. I don't think I want to go back there, but I don't know how to live with this. I don't know how to move past this."

I can't hold myself together anymore.

I dissolve into tears and Knox pulls me up onto his lap. He cradles me in his arms and cries with me as the rain outside continues to fall.

CHAPTER 33

I wake up to the sound of cars splashing through the water on the road outside.

I have spent the night snuggled close to Knox on the floor of the bar. At some point, he must have gotten up to blow out the candles. Light streams through the one window at the front of the room. His eyes are still closed, and my heart overflows with love as I study his face.

I run my fingers along the line of his jaw, then up to his lips. He groans and shifts slightly, but doesn't wake.

I smile and lean in to kiss his neck. I kiss him gently, my lips traveling up and down his neck, then across his cheek and jaw. When my warm lips touch his, his eyes flutter open and meet mine. My heart skips and I know I have found someone very special. I know he understands me and he isn't judging me.

He loves me.

He would never hurt me.

I close my eyes and press my lips to his. Our kiss deepens and he pulls me fully on top of him. My hands run through his hair and he parts his lips and runs his tongue across my bottom lip. His arms wrap tightly around me, pressing our bodies close.

This is what we've been waiting for. Whatever wall was there between us, holding us back from moving forward, is gone in the new morning light.

I have never felt so close to anyone in my life.

I break free of the kiss and bite his lip, then descend to his chin, his jaw, his neck.

He moans and takes my head in his hands. I look up to find him looking at me with such passion, it takes my breath away.

"I love you," he says.

I feel his words all the way down to the deepest part of my heart. "I love you, too."

"Where do we go from here?" He swallows and licks his lips. "I want you so badly, but I don't want to rush you."

"I want to be with you, too," I say. My heart is pounding. "But at the same time, it's hard because those memories are tied to sex, which makes it complicated. I don't want to freak you out if I have a memory that makes me need to stop or whatever."

He takes my hand and brings it to his lips. He softly kisses the skin along my knuckles.

"Then we'll take it slow," he says. "I'm going to listen to you and if you need to stop or slow things down, or if you're just not ready yet, I'm okay with that. I'll never judge you, Leigh Anne. You don't ever have to worry about what I think of you or how I feel about you, because right now and for the rest of my life, I am going to love you with all that I am."

His words sink into my heart like a healing balm.

I kiss him again, then run my hand down his chest. I find the edge of his t-shirt and slip my hand underneath, exploring the warmth of his skin with my fingertips. His stomach shudders at my touch and he gasps. His hands pull my tank top into a fist and he arches upward, grinding his body against mine.

Our kisses are slow and deep, our hands taking their time, exploring every inch of exposed skin.

But I want more.

I slide off to the side, then run my finger under the waistband of his jeans. He moans and closes his eyes. My pulse thunders in my veins and I reach for his belt buckle. His hand reaches for mine, his eyes questioning.

"Are you sure?" he asks. "I can wait if you need to."

I smile. "I've never been more sure of anything in my life."

We undress each other slowly, taking our time with every moment. Every kiss. Every touch.

My body aches for him and when I can't take it any longer, I move on top of him, my legs straddling him, our eyes locked. He laces his hands in mine and I press them back against the floor by his head. His chest rises and falls beneath me, his breath catching as I lower myself onto him.

He moves slowly at first, making sure I'm comfortable, then as our passion rises, he moves his hands to my hips and thrusts deeper.

I surrender myself to him without fear, and with his body and his love, he begins to heal me in a way I never knew was possible.

CHAPTER 34

"I wish we could stay here forever," I say.

Knox has fixed a small picnic on top of the bar. Fruit, peanuts, trail mix, and juice.

"You'll probably change your mind about that when this place is filled with drunk people around midnight."

I laugh and start peeling an orange. "I do need to figure out where I'm going to stay for a while," I say. "At least until I can get my own place."

I know my parents are probably already freaking out about me not coming back home last night. I'll have to go back and get the rest of my things, eventually, but for now, I really don't want to see them. At least, not my mother.

"You can stay with me," he says, leaning across the bar to kiss my cheek.

I blush, thinking of what it would be like staying in his apartment. I haven't even been to his place before.

"Too bad the lake house isn't fixed up yet," I say. In my head, I'm already dreaming of living there with him someday. Our own little paradise outside of town and away from everything.

THE TROUBLE WITH GOODBYE

"It's getting there," he says. He takes my hand in his. "We could step up the work on the renovations if you want. I bet I could have it fixed up enough to at least have the basics like plumbing, electricity, a basic kitchen by the end of the summer if we put enough time into it."

I smile. "I like the idea," I say. "I could enroll here at FCU to finish school."

"Or if you want to go back to Boston, I could get an apartment there for a while," he says. "At least until you graduate."

"You'd do that for me?" I'm not used to someone really considering what I want and being willing to sacrifice something they love to make me happy. "I couldn't let you do that. There's no way you'd be able to afford a place big enough to work on your furniture designs."

"We'll see," he says with a smile.

I shake my head, but inside, I feel warm and happy. I realize a weight has been lifted from my shoulders. Just the act of telling and being heard has freed me of so much tension, and I feel stronger than I have in over a year. Instead of being locked in the past, I'm thinking of my future again. It feels really good.

I know I must look a mess with yesterday's wrinkled clothes and my hair still wild from sleeping, but Knox doesn't seem to care. Still, I need a shower and a change of clothes.

"When does your shift start tonight?" I ask.

"Six, I think, why?"

"What time is it now?" I grab his wrist and turn my head to the side so I can read his watch. Seven in the morning. Plenty of time. "Do you think we can head back to your apartment so I can get a shower and get cleaned up? That rain really did a number on my hair."

I lift up and take a look at my reflection in the mirror behind the bottles of liquor. My normally straight hair is frizzy and wild.

"I think you look gorgeous," he says.

"You're the only one," I say. "Come on, let's get out of here."

We clean everything up and head out through the back door. Knox has his arm around me and we're smiling as a flash pulls my attention away from his face.

A large crowd lines the area behind the bar. People are shouting and taking pictures. I lift my hand to the back of my neck and look around, trying to figure out what these people are all taking pictures of. Knox's arm tightens around my waist.

A microphone is shoved into my face and the panic takes my breath away.

The truth slams me back against the door.

They know.

CHAPTER 35

"Leigh Anne, is it true you filed a report with campus administration last year accusing actor Burke Redfield of sexually assaulting you?"

"Ms. Davis, are you familiar with Molly Johnson's lawsuit against Burke Redfield?"

"Excuse me, Ms. Davis, can you tell us if you plan to file official charges?"

"Are you and Molly Johnson working together to destroy the actor's career?"

The questions rattle by at lightning speed and my head swims. I can't figure out why this is happening. How the fuck did they find out? We did everything we could to keep this a secret. They can't possibly know.

Knox recovers faster than I do. He pulls me tight against him and pushes through the crowd, shielding me as best as he can from the photographers.

We're almost to his truck when a cold hand wraps around my arm and a sharp voice shouts in my ear. "Don't say a word, Leigh Anne." I turn to see my mother. Her head is ducked low and she's guiding me away from Knox. "Just keep your head down and walk."

My father appears out of nowhere and parts the sea of reporters while my mother pushes me forward, down the sidewalk, toward my father's car. The door opens and just before I'm pushed inside, I turn to look for Knox.

But he's already gone.

CHAPTER 36

My mother guides me to the couch and sits next to me, her hand clasping mine.

I'm so inside my own head right now, I barely notice that there are other people here until an unfamiliar voice booms through the hallway.

"I got him out of the way as soon as I could," he said. "He put up quite a fight, I'll tell you that. It might take some work to convince him to stay away. Do you want me to go talk to him?"

I lift my head and blink. I don't recognize the man, and I can't see who he's talking to. I know who he's got to be talking about, though, and I don't like it one bit.

"Who is that?"

"That's Bernard Hunter. He works for Mr. Wright."

I open my eyes wide and for the first time since we got inside the house, take a real look around. My father is on the phone by the fireplace speaking in hushed tones. His forehead is creased with worry. Angela Simpson, my father's secretary, is typing furiously on her laptop at the kitchen table. I lean forward and see that Mr. Wright, Preston's father, is standing in the hallway with Bernard.

I stand and pull my hand away from my mother's. "What do you mean by convince him to stay away? Are you talking about Knox?"

My mother sighs heavily and comes to stand beside me. "Listen, Leigh Anne, this could get out of control very fast," she says. "It's bad enough that they found out about this at all, but how do you think it looks to have you coming out of some redneck bar in the early light of morning looking like white trash snuggled up close to some nobody?"

She might as well have slapped me across the face. Her words sting to the core of my heart. White trash? Is this what she thinks of me? "He's not nobody," I say. "I'm in love with him."

My mom grabs my arm and yanks me around to face her. "Now you listen to me, little girl. You have caused enough trouble for this family as it is without picking this moment to explore some rebellious phase you missed out on in your teens," she says. She releases my arm and smooths her skirt. "None of us wanted this to come to light, but now that they know, we've got to do everything we can to contain this story."

I don't like the sound of the word contain.

"If you had answered your phone this morning, you could have told us where you were and I could have sent your father to come get you," she says. She presses her hand to her forehead and paces the area beside me. "I wish we had found your car before they did. Now they have pictures of you with that boy and I'm sure they'll have a field day with that."

"Why do they care about Knox?" I ask. "He doesn't have anything to do with what Burke did to me."

My mother narrows her eyes at me in that way she has of making me feel about two inches tall. "Don't be stupid, Leigh

Anne. When it comes to cases of rape and sexual assault, it's not exactly a good idea to go making yourself look like a whore."

Anger flashes through me so hot and sudden that I raise my hand to her without thinking.

A strong hand reaches out to stop me before I make contact with her face and I struggle against him. My mother's eyes nearly pop out of her head. She backs away from me and covers her cheek as if she's felt the slap anyway. Does she really think she can just call me a whore without pissing me off?

"Let's just calm down for a minute here, folks." Tripp Wright, Preston and Penny's father, lets go of my wrist and puts his hand on my shoulder. He motions toward the couch. He has one of those low booming southern gentleman voices that commands the attention of a room, and everyone looks to him to solve this great problem.

I know I'm being handled, but I'm outnumbered so I sit down on the edge of the couch.

Wisely, my mother chooses to sit in the chair that's well out of my reach. I can barely bring myself to look at her.

"No, it wasn't ideal for you to come out of that bar with him," he says. "The press, in these types of cases, likes to look for any chance to stir the hornets' nest, so if they can find a way to discredit you in some way, they'll try to do it. We've all seen that happen with Molly already. Still, the story is very new and most of the big news stations haven't caught wind of this and gotten themselves down here yet. I've already got my family attorney out there explaining to the ones who are here now exactly why they should just forget that photo of you with Knox this morning. The story is that your car broke down in the storm last night and the two of you got stranded inside and fell asleep. I think they can be persuaded to keep the picture out of the papers just this once if we're lucky." He raises an

SARRA CANNON

eyebrow at me, as if to make sure I understand what he's telling me.

My shoulders drop and I swallow hard. "You're saying I can't see him again."

His mouth contorts into a look of sympathy and understanding, but I know it's an act. He wouldn't be here if he didn't have some personal interest in the whole thing. "It's for the best," he says. "Besides, if you really do care about that boy, you've got to see that it would be better for him if he wasn't dragged into this right along with you. Especially with his record."

I narrow my eyes at him. "He was a juvenile when he went to jail," I say. "His records are sealed."

He glances at my mother, then sits down next to me on the couch. "Technically yes, the details are kept under wraps, but that doesn't mean the press won't get hold of the story."

"He was a teenager who did some drugs," I say. "He's been clean for years. I don't see what the big deal is."

"The big deal is that he was incarcerated for aggravated assault." He pauses and I know there's more coming. I brace myself. "Of a woman."

I sit back against the couch. That can't be true. Knox wouldn't hurt a woman. "I don't believe you."

"I'm afraid it's true," my father says. He's finally off the phone and he comes to stand beside my mother. He puts a hand on her shoulder. "I saw the report myself."

I let my head fall into my hands. I remind myself to breathe. How could everything go from perfect to disaster in the snap of a finger? For the past year, I've been a floating ship with no anchor and no wind in my sails. The second I start to feel the stirring of hope, something has to come and bring me back down to the watery depths.

"The assault charges are bullshit," I say. "He told me the victim came forward afterward and told the truth."

"I don't know anything about that," Mr. Wright says. "I can have my people do some more digging, but it won't make any difference. The story will be spun any way the press wants to spin it. All they have to do is say you're dating a man who went to jail for assaulting a woman."

He doesn't have to spell it out for me. I see the red flags flying. If my name is going to be released by the press as a potential victim of the infamous Burke Redfield, the last thing I need is for my name to be linked to some guy who assaulted a woman. There won't be any easy way to explain that. The press will paint me as a reckless girl who makes bad choices and can't be trusted. They'll judge me in a heartbeat and discredit me faster than I can explain myself.

If I've learned anything while watching what Molly's been through, it's that the press is on Burke's side in this whole thing.

I want to curl up on the floor and go to sleep. I want to rewind six hours and convince Knox to run away with me. I could change my name. My face. My self.

But I can't. This is my life and, like it or not, I am going to have to face this.

I dig deep and gather strength from every corner of my being. I lift my head and see all eyes staring at me. Their expectations gather on my shoulders and I have no choice but to give them what they want. Anything else would just be too damn hard.

I take a deep breath, then square my shoulders.

"What do you want me to do?"

CHAPTER 37

"T he best thing to do right now is to lay low," Mr. Wright says. "We'll have your parents make a statement to the press. Leigh Anne, you need to stay inside the house for a few days until the story dies down a little. As long as you don't do anything to fuel the fire, there's a shot the story will die just as fast as it started."

"We all know that's not going to happen," my father says. "We need to find out who leaked this information in the first place and get a muzzle on them as fast as possible."

"We're working on that," Mr. Wright says. He stands and takes a place on the floor across from me where he can tower over us all. "Until we find the leak, though, we're going to have to try to manage the story from here. Without Leigh Anne's official statement to validate their story, they won't have anything to report but rumors and hearsay, and that isn't going to get them very far. Since there was no official report or complaint ever filed with the school's disciplinary committee, there shouldn't be much of a paper trail."

"What about the hospital?" Mom asks. She's wringing her

hands in her lap. "There will be a record somewhere of her being admitted for the initial rape kit."

"We'll need to see if we can get hold of that before the media does," he says. "Who else did you tell?"

"Campus police, my resident advisor, my roommate, the dean of students." The list is small, but big enough for me to have no idea who might have told.

"What's your roommate's name?" he asks. "Any chance she's the one who told the press? Maybe she has some desire to be a part of the news story?"

I shake my head. "Sophy's not like that," I say. "She would never tell anyone without talking to me first."

I go to get my phone from my bag, but it's not there. "I think I left my cell phone in my car."

"We'll need to get you a new phone," Mr. Wright says. "I'll get you one in my company name that you can use for emergencies, but you need to be very careful not to speak to anyone about the case over the phone or email."

"I'll still need my phone so I can get important numbers off of it," I say. I feel strangled. They're taking my phone away?

"I'll send Bernard to go pick up your car from the bar. You can grab your phone then, and we can switch them out later this afternoon," he says. "You'll need to be very careful who you speak with at this point, though. It would be best if you don't use the phone at all unless you have to."

"And no texts or calls with Knox," my mother says.

I tense, my teeth clenched. I need to get a message to Knox. I need to make sure he's okay and that he knows we might have to cool things off for a while, but that my feelings for him haven't changed. I have no idea how long this media attention will last, but I'm hoping it won't be more than a week or two before things can go back to normal. I don't want him to think I'm ignoring him. Especially not after what we shared.

I also want a chance to talk to Sophy about this. I need to make sure she didn't say something to someone accidentally.

"The other thing is that we're going to have to do everything we can to make Leigh Anne look as respectable and settled as we can," Mr. Wright continues. "The more we can convince them she's happy here and that there's no truth to this story about Burke Redfield, then the more they'll get bored and move on to a more sensational story with drama and intrigue."

I hear what he's saying, but I don't put it all together until the back door opens and Preston walks into the room. Suddenly, it all becomes clear.

Preston is playing the role of my knight in shining armor.

He meets my gaze and there is genuine concern in his eyes. I'm thankful for that much at least.

His father crosses over to him. "Preston, you got here just in time. Did you have any trouble getting through?"

"No sir," he says; his eyes still on me. "Bernard is keeping the driveway clear."

I wait for the master plan to unfold, but by this point, I have a pretty good idea what it's going to be.

I'm numb, caught between what was and what could have been.

"Later this afternoon, we'll have your mother and father issue a formal statement that while you did formerly attend the same school, you did not know Mr. Redfield or Molly Johnson and that you are not involved in any way in Ms. Johnson's lawsuit or the accusations she's making against the actor. The statement will also say that while you enjoyed your two years at the university, your affection for your high school sweetheart has brought you back home to Fairhope where you plan to enroll at FCU to complete your studies."

I close my eyes. Yes, I knew something like this was coming. I should have known the second I saw Mr. Wright in the house that the ulterior motive would be to push me back together with his son. This is what both our families have wanted all along, so why not use this unfortunate situation to bring us together?

My pain is merely an opportunity for a business merger.

I have no tears left to cry. I have only emptiness.

And the fear that everything I dreamed of just hours ago is now lost to me forever.

CHAPTER 38

W hen Mr. Wright is done explaining how I'm to behave and who I'm supposed to love for the rest of my life, I excuse myself and walk up the stairs to my room.

Bernard returned with my car and my phone earlier, and I plug my phone into the charger by the bed, then sit down and place my head in my hands. How could things have gotten so out of control so fast? The past year has been a series of impossible moments. Moments where I had to put on a brave face and soldier on no matter how broken I felt inside.

I survived that, and I will survive this too.

Somehow.

I strip my clothes from my body and run the shower as hot as possible, letting the hot water turn my skin pink and raw. Steaming, almost painful showers have become a ritual for me since that first shower the night I was raped. As long as I can feel the pain, I know I'm still alive. I'm still here fighting.

When I step out of the shower, I feel better.

My phone is charged enough to turn it on and check my

messages. I gasp when I see that I have over forty text messages and three hundred unread emails. I sink down onto my bed and quickly scan the messages, looking for two names. Sophy or Knox.

There's nothing from Knox, but Sophy's name pops up right away.

I find a frantic text message from her and my heart clenches inside my chest.

I need to talk to you. I think I fucked up. Please call me.

Then later:

Oh God, Leigh Anne, I'm so incredibly sorry. PLEASE call me. I need to talk to you.

The words break my heart. I know she would never do anything to intentionally hurt me, but regardless of intention, the end result is still the same.

My finger hovers over the phone, but I'm unsure how to respond. I don't want to call her or even hear her excuses right now. I just want to know who she told and why.

I finally type.

Was it you?

I already know the answer, but I'm hoping it will come with some kind of explanation.

The phone dings back seconds later.

Can I call you?

I tell her no. I tell her my phone is going to be turned off soon and she might not be able to reach me for a while. I tell her I want to know what happened.

Hard to explain over text. I volunteered for an event and Molly was there. We talked. I told her your story, but not your name. She figured it out on her own. Not sure how. I just wanted her to know she wasn't alone.

The messages come through and some level of relief passes through me. Sophy may have shared my story, but she didn't betray me. Not really. She didn't give Molly my name and hang me out to dry on purpose. Molly, or more likely her attorney, must have followed the paper trail. What little of it there was, anyway.

Are you okay? I never meant to hurt you.

I close my eyes.

Am I okay? I don't even have an answer for her, so I lay the phone down on the bed and walk away. I am just pulling on my shirt when someone knocks on my bedroom door.

I fling the door open expecting it to be my mom. I really don't want to talk to her right now or hear her bullshit.

But it isn't my mother. It's Preston.

My eyes widen and I pull my shirt the rest of the way down and tuck my wet hair behind my ears.

"Hey," he says. "I don't want to intrude if you need more time to process all this, but I'd really like to talk to you."

His expression seems genuine and his voice is soft and comforting. I have no idea if it's real or if it's another one of his acts. I guess now is as good a time as any to try to figure out if Preston is really going to be on my side in all this.

I step aside and motion for him to come in. He walks past me. I shut the door behind him, then lean back against it, arms crossed in front of my chest.

He sits down on the edge of my bed and looks down at his feet. "I had no idea," he says.

"About what? That your father had plans to force us back together?"

His eyebrows cinch together and he shakes his head. "I had no idea what happened to you at school," he says. "But no, I didn't know my father's plan, either. He just called me and told me to get over to your house as soon as I could. I saw the rest on the news."

I press my eyes closed. No wonder I have so many messages already. Some version of this story has already hit the news.

I want to fall into a heap on the floor, but the person I most need to comfort me isn't here. I refuse to fall apart in front of anyone but Knox. No one else will make me feel loved and comforted the way he did.

Instead, I stand. I survive.

"So it's really true?" he asks.

"No, I just lied about all of this to get my face on the news," I say, sarcasm rising to my tongue like a viper. It's the story they've run about Molly for weeks now and it pisses me off every time I see it. As if any woman wants to go through all this on purpose.

"That's not what I mean," he says. He stands and tries to put his hand on my shoulder.

I don't want him to touch me. I don't want to be touched by anyone right now. Especially someone who has no idea what I'm really going through.

"I haven't seen the news to see what story they're running, but yes, I imagine it's mostly true," I say. I'm torn between wanting to turn on the news and watch the whole thing unfold and wanting to throw my TV out the window.

Preston shakes his head and runs his hand through his hair. "God, Leigh. I don't even know what to say." He looks up. "If I had known, I never would have..."

His voice trails off and I think there's actual guilt in his tone.

"I know," I say. "That night was all about my issues, not yours. I got scared and overreacted."

"Still, I'm so sorry," he says. "I didn't mean to push you. I just thought things were the same between us, you know? Like we could pick up where we left off."

Is that what he still wants? Is he actually expecting me to go through with this plan?

"I know things haven't been easy for you," he says, turning to face me squarely. "And I know this media coverage is going to make your life hell for a while, but I promise I'm going to do everything I can to shield you from it."

I shake my head. He's so used to being able to fix everything with money and influence. He has no idea what this is really like for me. I'm so tired of everyone completely missing the point. No one here is really thinking about how the actual rape may have affected me. All they care about is the press and how much it will surely ruin my life if everyone finds out. What will they think of me? That's the only question that seems to matter to anyone.

"So you're on board with this plan of your father's?" I ask.

"Absolutely," he says. "Leigh Anne, you know I love you, right? I've always loved you."

"What about Bailey?"

He shrugs. "She'll understand," he says. "She already knows anyway, really. She's not stupid."

I want to ask what about Knox, but I already know what about Knox. They want to sweep him under the rug like trash and make sure he never speaks to me again. They'll do everything they can to keep us apart.

I can't let that happen.

"Preston, I need to tell you something."

He stands and walks toward the door, then turns back to me, sadness in his eyes. He waits, but I think he already knows what I'm going to say.

"I really appreciate this, but I don't want you to get the wrong idea," I say. "I'm in love with someone else."

He nods. "I know you care about Knox," he says. "I can't say I completely understand why, but I've seen the two of you together. I see the way you look at him sometimes. You used to look at me like that."

Did I? I never loved him the way I love Knox, but there's no use rubbing salt on his wounds.

"Knox... he's not the right guy for you, Leigh. I know that's not what you want to hear right now, and I know you don't believe me, but that's okay," he says. "I know I've hurt you in the past, but this time I'm going to prove to you just how much I love you. I'm going to be here for you and I'm going to stand by you through this. With my family's name behind this, the press won't dare run your name into the ground."

I'm touched by his words, but he's right. This is not what I want to hear right now.

"We had something special once," he says. "Maybe we can find that again. We're meant to be, you and me."

He gives me a small smile, but I can't return it. I'm sure he just thinks I'm going through something. Like my mother says, this is just a phase, right?

But it's not like that and none of them understand.

"I'm going to go ahead and pick up that new phone for you and bring it by later this afternoon, if that's okay," he says. "I thought I'd pick up some movies, too. Maybe some of your old favorites? We can watch movies all night and just chill. Like old times."

I smile and nod, playing my part. "Just like old times," I say.

But all I can really think about is how I'm going to get a message to Knox.

CHAPTER 39

After days of being sequestered in my parent's house, I have finally come up with a plan that just might work.

My parents insisted I quit my job, but I wouldn't hear of it. I told them that if they really wanted me to look happy and settled here in Fairhope, then they couldn't ask me to quit. How would it look? I needed to continue with my normal activities. Mr. Wright's own words. They couldn't argue.

Maria agreed that in light of the news bomb, she'd give me some time off, but that she expects me back within a week.

My mother claims that having a job as a waitress makes me look common, but I have no idea why she thinks being common is such a bad thing. I don't think plastering it over CNN that I am working at a steak house waiting tables will make anyone gasp and point their finger at me. She's just using this to control me in every way, and I'm not going to allow it.

Besides, the decision has been made whether she likes it or not, and by the time a week has passed, I'm aching to get out of this house.

I pull on my black work pants, white button-up and my boots and head downstairs to grab something quick to eat before I head out.

My mom is sitting in the kitchen watching TV. She changes the channel as soon as I enter the room, as if she's trying to hide the news from me. All they're doing is replaying the same story and pictures over and over, but she still watches it just to make sure they haven't figured out anything new. It's been eight days and already the story about me is fading since they don't have any real confirmation or declaration from me.

I'm sure they were all hoping I'd come forward with some sensationalized story, but I'm not ready to take that step. And if I do, I won't sensationalize anything. I'll tell the truth exactly as it happened.

"Why are you dressed like that?" My mother has a nasty scowl on her face.

I'm sure she was just thinking it was an ugly outfit at first, but then the truth dawns on her and anger flashes across her features.

"Are you seriously going back to that awful job?" she asks. "I don't think it's such a good idea. We don't need to give the press anything to report. Plus, I don't want them harassing you while you're there."

I open the fridge and take out a bag of baby carrots and some ranch dip.

"Bernard's been assigned to keep an eye on me," I say. What more could they really expect of me? "I have done everything you've asked of me, including staying away from the man I love. You're not going to take this away from me, too. We already talked about this."

She shakes her head and grabs a towel to wipe up the spilled coffee. "You should at least wait until after the press conference. I'm going to call your father," she says. "Maybe he can talk some sense into you."

I roll my eyes. "What's your problem with me working? You've been against it from the start, even before the news found out about me," I say. "Why are you so against it? It makes no sense to me at all."

"I think you're being careless," she says.

"And I think you're being fucking ridiculous."

She pulls her head back and her eyes pop open so wide, I think her eyeballs are going to pop out of their sockets. "You are not allowed to talk to me like that, little girl."

I snort and shake my head. "You just don't get it, do you?" I say.

"Get what?"

"That I'm not a little girl, anymore," I say. "I don't have to do what you say."

"Don't say that," she says. "We all need to stick together right now."

There's fear in her voice, but what she's really afraid of is losing control of me. I think that's the real reason she never wanted me to have a job. If I have my own money, I have some level of independence and she just can't handle it.

"When you're ready to start supporting me instead of judging me, let me know, okay?"

I grab the bag of carrots from the table and storm out the back door.

She doesn't bother following me.

CHAPTER 40

The television over the bar is set to the news again tonight, and I see my face flash across the screen several times with questions across the bottom of the screen like "How many victims are there?" and "Will Leigh Anne come forward?" I want to grab one of the beer bottles off the counter and sling it toward the big screen.

"Hey, Colton, can we get a channel change?" Jenna shouts. She puts her arm around me even though I'm about four inches taller than she is.

Colton sees me standing there, then apologizes and changes it to ESPN instead. A couple of people groan, but some cheer and in the end, no one really cares anyway. "Sorry, Leigh Anne, I didn't realize you were coming back tonight."

"Thanks," I say as we make our way back toward the kitchen. It's not too busy tonight, so we have some down time between tables. "My mom watches that shit all the time, but every time I come in the room, she either turns it off or changes it right away, like I'm a child."

"Maybe she's just trying to protect you."

I roll my eyes and throw my tray on the counter in the back. "The only thing my mother cares about protecting is her own reputation."

Jenna points toward the back door and I shrug. I follow her out back and we sit on top of the picnic table. I look around, double checking that there are no reporters around.

More importantly, I look to make sure Bernard Hunter isn't anywhere he can hear us.

She lights up a cigarette. "I tried to stop by your house after the news hit," she says. "Did your dad tell you?"

I shake my head. "They're barely speaking to me unless it's to give me orders about how to act," I say. I bite my lip. I hate to bring Jenna into this, but she's been a good friend to me. I really need her right now. I'm just not sure how to ask her what I need to ask her.

"I just can't believe that asshole hurt you like that. He deserves to burn in hell," she says. She takes a long drag of her cigarette, then waves the smoke away from me. The wind carries it away. "Don't get me wrong. I don't blame you one bit for not speaking up. I don't think I could really do it, either. Especially not with someone famous like that, where the press is going to be watching your every move. Still, I bet you're glad someone else spoke up. I mean, if you've kept quiet about it, how many others are there? It's good there's a chance he'll still go to prison for what he did."

I grab her hand and squeeze. "You didn't even ask me if it was true," I say.

"I didn't have to," she says. "I could see it in your eyes the moment I first laid eyes on you."

I stare down at my feet and sadness washes over me. If someone who just met me could see it, why couldn't my family see it? Why did they insist on acting like this was some kind of nuisance?

"I'm really sorry you had to go through that," she says. "No one should ever have to go through something like that."

"No, they shouldn't," I say.

I think about Molly Johnson. If I hadn't let my parents and the school administration shut me up, would she have been raped? Or could I have stopped it? What if I had spoken up first? I could have saved her from this, and who knows how many other girls?

I shake my head. I can't think like that. It's not my fault he hurt them.

"Hey." Jenna leans down so she can see my eyes. I look up and she smiles a little. "Are you doing okay?"

I suck in a tense breath. "Not really," I say. "But I know a way you could help me feel a whole lot better."

"I'll do anything," she says. She throws her cigarette into a bucket sitting near the table. "All you have to do is ask."

I stand up and move in front of her, getting as close as I can. "They haven't let me so much as send a text message to Knox to explain to him what's going on," I say. "They're terrified the news will pull his story about going to jail and use it as fuel to fan the fire in this thing. But I have to talk to him."

"What can I do?" she asks.

I explain my plan and she nods. "No problem," she says with a smile. "Tomorrow night?"

"Yes," I say, then take her hand. "Thank you, from the bottom of my heart. I don't want to get you mixed up in this, but I wasn't sure who else to turn to. "

"I'm here for you however you need," she says.

"That means more than you can know," I say. "I've been locked away in that house for a week thinking it was miserable, but tonight's been tough too. It's hard seeing the looks and hearing the whispers as I walk by. It's like, suddenly this story defines me."

"Not to me, it doesn't," she says. She squeezes my hand. "To me, it's just one layer of many. We're all somewhat the sum of our experiences, you know? But each individual event can only define us if we let it. If you don't want this to define you, then don't let it."

I stand and shake my head. "I can't control what other people think of me."

"It's not about learning how to control it. Most of life is out of our hands," she says. "The real key is how we react to the things we can't control. You can't control what people think of you or what they believe happened, but you can control how you respond to it."

I want to tell her that in my life right now, my parents have taken control of how I respond. Mr. Wright has had more say in my reaction than I have. But before I get the chance to continue the conversation, Maria sticks her head out the back door and motions for us to come inside.

Jenna turns and just before we get inside, she winks.

CHAPTER 41

The following night, my shift lasts forever. My feet ache and my head is throbbing.

All I can think about is Knox and whether he'll be understanding about this or whether he'll be pissed off at me. He has every right to be pissed, and I know it.

I finish putting plastic wrap on the salad dressings and shove them into the walk-in fridge, then join Jenna at the drink station. She's pulling the little caps off each dispenser and dropping them in a bucket of soda water.

"I thought tonight would never end."

She laughs. "Welcome to my world," she says. "I haven't had a day off in two weeks. It's all a blur at this point."

"Wow, two weeks?"

She nods. "I even worked a double shift the past two days. My feet are killing me," she says. "I have tomorrow off, thank god."

"Me too." My nerves dance inside my body, thinking of Knox waiting for me.

She loops her arm in mine. "So we're good for you spending the night at my place?" she asks in a whisper.

I nod. We walk together toward the lockers and start getting ready for checkout.

"I have to know how you managed to pull that off when your parents are up your ass about everything these days."

"I just told them I needed a break and I wasn't asking their permission," I say, leaning against the wall.

Her eyes grow wide and her jaw drops to the floor. "Kick ass," she says. "You seriously told them that?"

I shrug. "In so many words," I say with a laugh. "They agreed, on the condition that my watchdog, Mr. Hunter, could sit outside in his car to make sure I was okay."

She raises an eyebrow and tilts her head to the side. "Good thing we planned ahead."

CHAPTER 42

I can hardly stand still as I wait for Jenna to get her key in the lock and open the door already.

As soon as she does, I run in and drop my bag on the floor. Knox throws his arms around me and lifts me up into the air. I bury my head in his neck and inhale the scent of him.

Behind me, Jenna giggles and claps her hands. She disappears into the kitchen as Knox pulls me into a kiss.

"I missed you so much," I say.

"I missed you, too." He takes my hands in his. "I've been so worried about you. Some asshole pulled me away from you that day, and I couldn't get to you before they put you in that car and took you away. I have tried everything I could think of to get in to see you, but your parents have that place locked up like a jail. I'm guessing they turned your phone off, too. When I call it, all it does is give a busy signal."

"They took my phone away," I say.

"I'm going to give you two lovebirds some privacy," Jenna says. She's got a six pack of beer, a bag of chips, and a box of Hot Tamales in her hands. "I'll be back in my bedroom watching a movie if you need anything. Otherwise, mi casa es su casa. And fyi, the couch pulls out into a bed."

I laugh, but don't take my eyes off Knox.

Jenna pecks a kiss on my cheek, then rushes off toward the back room and shuts the door.

I lift up on my tiptoes and wrap my arms around Knox's neck. We press our foreheads together and just stare at each other for a minute. My heart is beating wildly and I want nothing more than to smother him in kisses.

"I'm so glad you're here," I say.

He pulls me toward the couch, and lowers me onto his lap. "How are you handling all this? Do you have any idea how the press found out?"

"Mr. Wright and my dad have been researching the trail all week," I say. "My roommate Sophy went to a sexual abuse awareness event on campus and ran into Molly. She told her she knew someone who had also been raped by Burke, but didn't give her any details. From there, Molly's attorney tracked down a nurse who worked at the university clinic when I was admitted. It's all a big mess."

He takes my hand and kisses my palm softly. "What are you going to do? Have you figured it out?"

"Have you been watching the news?" I ask.

"Some," he says. "When I'm not too angry to stomach it."

"They've been calling me a coward," I say, tears filling my eyes. I take a deep breath. For the past week and a half, I've refused to let the tears fall. I haven't wanted my parents to see me rattled by this. But with Knox, it's different. I feel freer with him than with anyone. "Some of the things they've said are true, but other things are total bullshit. Like one channel was reporting that I'd supposedly taken a million dollar payoff to keep my mouth shut. Someone online accused me of getting an abortion. It's out of control."

Knox is quiet, and I can tell he wants to say something. He keeps opening his mouth, but then changing his mind. My stomach twists.

"What?"

He takes in a deep breath. "Have you considered coming forward and just telling the truth about what happened?" he asks. "I mean, now that it's already in the news, what do you have to lose?"

I tense. "You sound like Sophy. She's been urging me to come forward ever since the beginning. Or at least, she was before my parents banned me from having any contact with her." I think about Sophy's reasons and guilt floods through me all over again. "Sophy says there's strength in numbers and now that someone else has come forward, it's much more likely the administration and the police will really listen to what we have to say."

"She has a good point," he says.

I sit up, scooting off of his lap. "I'd be lying if I said it hasn't crossed my mind," I say. "Of course, there's a part of me that wants to come forward. But at the same time, I don't honestly know if I can handle it. It isn't like I'd just have to tell my story once and be done with it. Look at Molly. She's probably told her story a dozen times to police, her attorney, reporters, which means she has to relive what happened to her over and over and over. And when it comes to trial, she'll have to sit across from him and go through the whole thing again, right there in front of him. She's opening herself up to everyone's judgment and scrutiny. People are attacking every single choice she's made along the way, from the guys she dated in high school all the way down to the clothes she was wearing that night. I don't want that to be my life."

"I can understand that," he says. "But I want to make sure

this is really your choice and not something your parents are deciding for you."

"I know," I say with a sigh. "I'm thinking of you and me in all this, too."

He looks confused. "What do you mean?"

I fidget. I know this is going to be a tough conversation, but it's something we need to talk about. "If I come forward with the truth, there's going to be a lot of press. There will be tons of interviews, trips back up to Boston, and everything that comes along with this," I say. "If you and I are together, they won't just be pulling my choices apart. They'll be looking into your past and your choices too."

He closes his eyes and leans his head back against the couch. "My record at juvie will come up," he says. "And you're afraid it'll make you look bad."

I swallow a thick lump in my throat, but it won't go away. "Mr. Wright said you were arrested in Chicago for hitting a woman," I say. "Is that true?"

He clenches his jaw. "How did he find out about that?"

I stare at him. "He said that even though the records are technically sealed, there are people who know about it who are willing to talk."

He sighs and stands. His hands open wide, then tense into fists. "Fuck," he says, then punches a fist against the bar.

My heart sinks down into the depths of my stomach.

"Tell me," I say. "I need to know."

"First of all, I didn't beat up a woman," he says. He can't stop moving. "I already told you those charges were bullshit. You know I wouldn't hurt a woman."

"But that's what they arrested you for, right? In part? I need to know the whole story."

I wait. After a long silence, he finally relaxes his shoulders and starts talking.

"When I got to Chicago, my life was complete hell," he starts. "I already explained a lot of it to you, but I didn't tell you the whole story. Several years after he abandoned my mother and got a great job as a partner with a high-profile investment company in Chicago, he met Dawn. She was twelve years younger than him, which made her closer to my age than his. They had two little kids, twin girls, right before I moved in and yeah, everything seemed perfect for them. They lived in this giant mansion just outside of the city, drove the best cars, wore the best clothes, all that shit. Dawn never really talked to me much the first few years I lived there. She was a parrot of my father. Whatever he said, she stood behind him. I thought she was mindless, so I guess I never paid that much attention to her.

"Then, one night I came home really fucked up and high on meth. I walked in on him beating up on her. They were in the living room and I didn't even see her at first. I just thought he was standing there in the dark like a dumbass. But then I heard her crying. He didn't even take his eyes off me when he kicked the shit out of her and told her to shut up. I walked around the corner, trying to figure out what the hell was going on and there she was."

"Dawn?"

He nods. "She was in a heap on the floor, blood pouring from her lip, clutching her side. She was sobbing and he kept yelling at her to shut the fuck up."

I bring my hand to my mouth, listening but not wanting to believe it.

"I went insane. Here he was, always pretending to be such a perfect man while all this time he'd been abusing his wife," he says. "No wonder she never dared to disagree with him. No wonder my mother fucking kicked him out of her life. It all made sense to me, even in my spaced out mind at the time. I called him a piece of shit and told him if he touched her one more time, I would kill him. You know what he did?"

My mind races with the possibilities, thinking his father probably provoked him.

"He laughed at me. He said he'd teach me not to threaten him." Knox leans against the wall and puts his head in his hands.

"He hit you?"

Knox shakes his head. "Worse," he says with a distorted laugh. "He called the cops."

My mouth falls open and I try to piece it all together.

"He told them I'd come home fucked up out of my mind and when Dawn told me to leave, I beat the crap out of her," he says. When he looks up at me, his eyes are red. "Dawn backed up the story and the police carted me away once and for all. Of course, I tested positive for drugs and I'd gotten in a couple fights recently, so my hands looked like I'd been beating on someone. That was all they needed. Since I was only fifteen, they put me in juvenile detention center for three years with plans to reevaluate me at eighteen. I didn't see my father again after that."

"Oh, my god." I stand and go to him. I put my hand on his arm, but he's tense and angry and he pulls away. "I had no idea you'd been through all that. Why didn't you tell me?"

"I was going to," he says. "But this whole news thing blew up right when we were really starting to open up to each other. It honestly never even occurred to me that anyone would try to use my past against you in all this. Besides, I told you, Dawn retracted her story just before my eighteenth birthday."

"She told the truth?"

"She told the court that my father had lied and that he had been the one who hit her."

My eyes widen. "She wasn't scared what he would do to her for telling the truth?"

Knox turns and his eyes are sad and haunted. "Not at that point," he says. "My father was dead."

I swallow and draw in a breath. "What happened to him?"

He stares down at his feet. "He hit one of the twins," he says. He looks up at me. "And Dawn shot him."

CHAPTER 43

I'm in shock. I had no idea he'd been through so much.

"What happened to her?"

"She was eventually convicted of voluntary manslaughter," he says. "His abusive behavior became the centerpiece of the trial. The jury believed she was abused, but they couldn't overlook the fact that she'd planned the whole thing in such detail. When he left for work earlier that morning, she sent the kids to her sister's and moved his favorite recliner right in front of the door, where she could have a clean shot. Then she started drinking vodka and popping Xanax until he walked in the door at six that evening. She shot him five times before he even made it across the threshold. A neighbor heard the shots and called the cops, but by the time the paramedics arrived, he was already dead."

"What about the twins?"

"They went to live with her sister's family," he says. "I try to go up and see them when I can, but they were so young when this all went down, they don't really remember me or our father."

I stare ahead, my face blank. I can't even imagine how hard this all must have been on Knox. To go from a life where he was happy with his mom to having to deal with an abusive father, being thrown in jail for something he didn't even do, and then finally to have his father murdered and his step-mother thrown in jail? It's just too much.

I lean against him and kiss the bare skin on his arm just below where his t-shirt sleeve hits. His muscle is tight and I feel it ripple beneath my hand. "I'm sorry."

"It's okay," he says. "I've had years to deal with it all. I honestly thought I'd left it all behind me when I moved here. Knowing it could mess things up for you makes me angry all over again."

I close my eyes and pull him closer to me. I'm caught between two paths, and I have no idea what to do. "If I come forward and tell the truth about what happened to me, there's a better chance he'll actually go to jail for what he did," I say. "But adding my name to the trial could push it back months. Maybe years. I have no idea. In the meantime, the press is going to be looking for juicy stories to splatter all over the front pages and if you and I spend any time together at all, they're going to find out about your past."

He rests his chin on top of my head. Our arms are wrapped around each other.

"If I stay quiet or even deny it outright and decide to let it go, we can move on with our lives."

"But Molly Johnson might lose her case against him and he'll be free to keep doing this to other women."

"Yes," I say, my voice a whisper.

He holds me tight for a long time before we part. "What do you want to do? I'm going to support whatever decision you make," he says. "I love you, no matter what."

"I want you," I say. I bury my face in his chest. "But at the same time, I don't know if I can stand up there and lie about this. If I say nothing happened that night, I'm betraying myself in a way. I'm not sure I'll ever be able to get over that."

"Then you have to speak up," he says. He puts his hand under my chin and lifts my eyes to him. "You have to let your voice be heard."

"I don't want to lose you," I say, my lip trembling.

"You won't," he says. "I'll wait for you, as long as it takes. We'll get through this."

Tears well up in my eyes and he frowns.

"What? Is there something else?"

"Sit down," I say, pulling him to the couch.

He sits next to me, his hand in mine, and I tell him about Preston.

CHAPTER 44

"It makes sense," he says when I'm through explaining the Wrights' plan for me. "Either way, if you decide to speak out against Burke or not, it can only make you look better in the eyes of the press if you have Preston's family there beside you."

I put my head in my hands. "I was sort of hoping you'd tell me I was crazy for even considering it."

I feel lost. Hopeless.

Knox places his hand on my knee and kisses the top of my head. "I just hate that my shitty past is going to make things harder for you," he says. "I wish I could go back and change it, but I can't. And they're right, the press will jump all over you the same way they did with Molly. I don't want to burden you with that."

"I don't know what to do."

"You don't have to make a decision right now, do you?" he asks.

I stand and shake my head. "Yeah, actually I do."

His eyes question me.

"My family has called a press conference for tomorrow on the steps of the courthouse," I say. "I'm to give my official statement to the press."

"Tell them you aren't ready." He stands and paces. "They can't force you to talk. Just tell them you need more time."

I shake my head. "There is no more time," I say. "I got a call from Molly's attorney. He said there is still a chance right now to add me as a second victim. He said something about having to drop the initial case and reinstate the charges, now with these additional charges added on. It was a lot of legal jargon I didn't really understand, but if I'm going to come forward with the truth, I'm running out of time. And if I'm going to deny it, I'd rather just get it over with."

We stand there in silence, the truth of our situation becoming clearer by the second.

"My family wants me to deny everything. They think that if I don't file charges and go through a trial, I'll be able to just move on. And if I show the press I'm happily settled here in Fairhope with my Preston by my side, the public will lose interest in the story and the press will feel obligated to move on rather than provoke a wealthy family like the Wrights."

I rattle off the reasons, thinking out loud.

"But if I tell the truth and decide to move forward with official charges, my family believes it will at least take some of the heat off of us if the Wrights are there to throw their power and influence behind me. Of course, that means I have to be with Preston at least throughout this trial, and you and I won't be able to see each other again."

Knox runs a trembling hand through his hair.

"Or," I turn to him, "I could just say fuck it and let them say what they will about us. About my choices."

He comes to me, his eyes stormy. "I don't ever want to be a source of pain for you," he says. "I love you too much to ask you to do that for me. Think about what that would mean for you. Preston's dad is right. The press will look at you like you're the kind of girl who does reckless things and makes poor choices."

I lean my head against his chest. This is an impossible choice, and I can't see clearly enough to know which way is right. If I say goodbye to him now, when we've just found each other, will I lose him forever?

"Which are you leaning toward?"

I close my eyes. "I don't want to lose you," I say. "Denying everything will get the press off my back sooner and maybe will bring us together faster."

He shakes his head. "But then you've publicly denied he ever did anything to you," he says.

And I love him for understanding. I love him for not being angry at me for considering all options.

He stops pacing and looks at me with such sorrow. "I'm not going to see you again for a while, am I?"

I shake my head, a tear escaping down my cheek.

There are no more words that need to be said between us. No matter what I choose to do tomorrow, this will be our last night together for a very long time. With the emotions of the possible trial and press involvement and the time apart, not even being able to talk, we both know our future is now completely up in the air.

He kisses me, hard and desperate. Together, we fall to our knees, clinging tight to what we have here and now.

I pull his shirt from his body, my fingers digging into his skin. I am desperate for him, but he takes my hands in his. He slows me down.

"I want to make this last," he says.

He turns me around so that my back is pressed against him. He runs his fingertips up my arms and a chill shudders through me. I lean my head to the side and he kisses my neck as his hands explore.

I lift my hand to his neck, then turn back to face him. Our kisses are slow. I take my time tasting him, exploring his tongue with my own. I pull his bottom lip into my mouth, teasing it with my teeth and he groans.

"I love the way you bite your lower lip when you're thinking or worried," I say.

He smiles. "I do that?"

"Mm-hmm." I kiss him again and we go deeper. I run my hand through his hair. His hand caresses the side of my breast and I lean into him, wanting him.

Every piece of me, body and soul, yearns for him.

He makes love to me then, and we savor each moment, knowing it may be our last.

CHAPTER 45

In the morning, I run.

I throw on an old pair of running shorts I find in the back of one of my drawers and take off just as the sun peeks over the horizon. Saying goodbye to Knox was one of the hardest things I've ever had to do, and I'm still not sure I've made the right choice.

I need to clear my head before I can face those cameras today.

And since there's no rope swing and no Knox, I run.

I follow my old path. The one that leads through the woods behind my house, down along the creek, toward the park. I used to run this path every single morning before class when I was in high school.

The whole run takes about an hour, but this morning I wish it was longer.

I wish I could run forever and avoid this press conference altogether.

As my feet hit the familiar wooded path, I concentrate on my breathing, pushing everything else from my mind. I force my shoulders to relax. It's been so long since I ran, but my legs are strong. I am going to need that strength today. Some instinct deep inside takes over. With every foot-fall, I open my lungs a little deeper, letting the air really flow into me. Even this early in the morning, the humidity is thick and the air is hot. It clings to me like a veil, covering me from head to toe.

I am in mourning.

As I run, I mourn for the life that could have been. The joy that was stolen from me when I was just truly learning to discover it on my own. I mourn for the other girls who might be going through the exact same thing right now, their voices strangled by fear or duty or the disbelief of others.

My heart slams against my ribs and less than a mile in, my legs are burning, begging me to stop. But I can't. I need this.

Instead of slowing down, I run faster.

In Boston, I'd only run a little for the first few weeks of my freshman year. Once my classes really got going, I didn't have a lot of free time. I tried going to the gym and running on the treadmill with a book in front of me, but it wasn't the same. I eventually gave up on it, only avoiding the freshman fifteen because of all the walking I had to do from one class to another.

Until this moment, I hadn't realized just how much I'd missed it. The release. The burn.

I push harder. Faster.

But I can't outrun the past. Or the future.

Unable to breathe, I slow to a stop and bend over, resting my hands on my knees and gasping. Tears of frustration and loss flow down my cheeks.

And I let them fall.

The quiet woods shelter me as I break down. I stand up straight and place my hands on my hips, turning in a circle as sobs rock my body.

How could I have let this happen to me? How could I have

been so incredibly stupid? I want to go back there to that night and have a chance to make different choices. To say no to ever going with Burke in the first place.

I slam my fist against a tree, then lay my head on its bark.

Knox is right. I have to learn to stop blaming myself for this. No matter my choices, Burke had no right to do what he did. He's the only one to blame in this, and I have to find a way to quiet the negative voice that keeps telling me it's all my fault.

The real question I need to ask is what's the best way for me to heal? How do I move forward? What do I really want?

I draw in a long breath, a lingering sob shaking me as the breath enters my body.

I can do this. It's going to be okay.

I lift the bottom of my shirt and wipe away what's left of my tears.

I stretch my sore legs, take a stronger breath, then keep running.

CHAPTER 46

I take my time getting ready.

I still have no idea what I'm going to say at the press conference. As the minutes tick away, the knots in my stomach grow more intense.

I'm torn between several possible futures, and I'm not sure I want any of them. It's too hard. Too uphill. Am I strong enough for this? Am I really ready to face what happened to me?

When I get out of the bathroom, there's a navy dress laid out on my bed. Pearls. Off-white and tan heels. As if it isn't enough that they're planning what I should say, my mother also apparently thinks I'm not capable of choosing my own clothes.

I run my finger along the bodice of the dress. I haven't worn this since high school. I hate this dress. The hem is too long and makes me look like a goodie two-shoes little girl. This is how my mother still sees me and the image makes me sick to my stomach. She still refuses to acknowledge the fact that I've grown up. She refuses to accept that my experiences have changed me.

I wonder if we'll ever be able to sit down and have a real conversation or connect in any real way.

I cross to the closet and stand looking at my clothes for a full ten minutes before I finally choose a black pencil skirt and a simple teal blouse. Instead of pearls, I wear the silver necklace my grandmother gave me before she passed away.

Believe.

The message is a good one for today. Not because I need them to believe my story.

But because I need to believe in myself.

CHAPTER 47

The sun is shining high in the sky as we reach the steps of the courthouse.

A podium is set up in the center of the stairs and reporters are casually talking, their prime spots already claimed. Several of them hold microphones or cameras. A few hold small notebooks, ready to immortalize my words in print.

My palms sweat and my head swims.

I'm not sure I'm ready for this.

My mother grabs my hand and I recoil at her touch. The fact that she gets to stand up here with me, and Knox doesn't, gives me an empty feeling in my stomach. What I'm doing today is important, but it's still a show. To the people watching this on TV or reading about it in the paper, I'll just be another face in the drama. Almost entertainment.

The real struggle is in the day-to-day, not these sensational-ized moments. I know by speaking out, I also open myself up to judgment and accusation and even resentment. But after keeping quiet for so long, I know that speaking out and telling my story is the only way I'm ever going to find a level of peace with what he did to me.

Preston and his father come to stand by my side. Preston hugs me and I hug him back. I may not have a real future with him, but I do appreciate what he's willing to do for me.

Mr. Wright has a small stack of index cards in his hand and he passes them to me.

Confused, I look down and begin reading.

Thank you all for being here. Although I appreciate the struggle of women like Molly Johnson, I am in no way linked to the events in Boston. It's true that I did meet Burke Redfield my freshman year at the university. We went out on two separate occasions, but our relationship never progressed beyond that, and I have not spent any time with him since.

My decision to leave Boston had nothing to do with Mr. Redfield. In fact, I came home to be reunited with my high school sweetheart, Preston Wright, and the two of us are hoping to be engaged by summer's end.

I can't read any more. "This is what you expect me to say today?"

"There's another set of cards," Mr. Wright says. "If you feel you need to press formal charges against Burke Redfield, the Wright family will stand behind you every step of the way. Our attorney is aware of the situation and he's ready to work with the attorneys in Boston to give you the best possible team should you decide to move forward."

He pauses, then shares a look with my mother.

"I have to be honest with you, though." He puts his hand on Preston's shoulder. "We all really feel the best thing for you right now is to deny any involvement and move on from this once and for all. If you press charges, it's going to be a circus around here. Your life will be consumed with this for months. Years, maybe. This trial will follow you for the rest of your life,

Leigh Anne. Think about that, now. Another woman has already pressed charges against this young man. His career is already ruined by this case. He's going to get what's coming to him one way or the other. Do you really need to let him steal any more of your life away by taking this thing to court?"

I swallow hard and look at the expectant faces of my parents and the Wrights. The argument makes sense. He's right about what will happen to me if I step forward as a victim. A survivor. But the flaw in their logic is believing that if I stay silent, this will all disappear. As if this is merely one minor event in my past that can be swept under the rug and forgotten.

No matter what I choose here today, what happened to me has become a part of who I am. There's no escaping it.

All I can do now is embrace it.

I nod and hold the cards obediently in my hand.

My mother's shoulders relax. "This will all be over in a few minutes," she says, squeezing my arm. "We can finally put this behind us."

I close my eyes and lean against the cool, smooth stone column.

When they come to get me, my mouth is dry and my pulse is racing.

I step in front of the bay of microphones and the cameras begin to flash.

I inhale. Exhale. I try to use my techniques, but my lungs are locked and my breaths are shallow.

I stare down at the notecards I've been given. I know it's not too late to follow their path for me. I can deny everything. Hide under the shelter of the Wright family's influence until this whole thing blows over.

I'm back on that ledge, a choice to make. Step back into a false sense of safety. Or step out into the unknown.

I'm so scared.

But then I think of Molly Johnson. I wonder if she's watching, her stomach in knots like mine.

I wonder if there are others.

I think of them and how maybe, a moment of courage from me today will give a voice to those who cannot speak.

Time moves in slow motion. I stare out at the sea of reporters, their hands lifted, waiting. My hands are trembling. My ears are ringing. My chest is tight.

Then, toward the back of the crowd, his eyes meet mine. Blue and clear and full of love.

And suddenly an image of our first night at the lake pops into my mind. Me, on a rope swing, flying into the darkness. No fear. Only faith.

I look down at the words written on the cards. Lies that stink of fear and shame.

I lay them down against the podium and look up at the waiting crowd.

And I make my choice.

CHAPTER 48

"Thank you all so much for coming," I say. My voice trembles slightly. I clear my throat and inhale an uneven breath. "My name is Leigh Anne Davis and I am a student at the same university as Burke Redfield and Molly Johnson. Although I have never met Ms. Johnson, I have, in fact, met Burke Redfield."

All eyes are fixed to my face. I swallow and my throat feels like sandpaper.

"Last year, just before spring break of my freshman year, Burke Redfield took me on a date." My hands are shaking, so I press them together tight. It takes every ounce of courage to speak the words. "He raped me."

The crowd breaks out in a roar. My mother reaches for my arm, but I pull away from her. I will not let her silence me.

I wait as the officials attempt to quiet the area.

I seek out Knox's eyes and he nods, encouraging me to keep going. Tears sting my eyes.

"I reported the assault through the proper channels at my university, submitted to a rape kit, was questioned by the authorities and the Dean of Students," I say. "After a limited investigation, I was told by the administration and by my own family that it would be in my best interest to keep all of our proceedings off the official record until a decision was made as to the validity of my claims. And after months of waiting, I was finally told there would be no official hearing."

As I speak, I find strength.

"The university swept any evidence under the rug and failed to make any of those reports available to me," I say. "They took away my voice, telling me further accusations would bring shame to both me and to my school. For a year and a half, I have lived with the pain of what happened to me without any support from my school. In the meantime, Burke Redfield has been free to continue attending school at the university, putting other women, like Molly Johnson, in danger.

"Today, I announce my intention to file official charges against Burke Redfield."

CHAPTER 49

I know there will be questions. Consequences.

And I will face them as best I can in the coming weeks and months.

But right now, all I want to do is feel Knox's arms around me.

I step away from the podium, ignoring the wave of noise at my back. I hand the notecards to Preston's father. Preston stands beside him. When I meet his eyes, he gives me a sad smile.

"I want you to know that I do appreciate what you were trying to do for me," I say. "But I need to do this on my own terms and in my own way. I need to tell the truth in order to move on, and I hope you can both understand that."

Preston pulls me into a hug. "I think you are very brave to do what you just did up there," he whispers in my ear.

I pull away and touch his face briefly. "Thank you for being here for me."

Preston's father reaches for my hand. "It's going to be a tough road ahead, but I know this had to be a very difficult choice for you to make," he says. "If you need any help, you just ask."

"I appreciate that," I say.

My mother's expression is much less understanding. Tears stream down her face and she's leaning against my father, as if she couldn't possibly be expected to stand on her own at a moment like this.

She shakes her head and wipes her eyes with a tissue. "I don't understand this at all," she says. "After everything we did to protect you from this, you just throw it all away in the blink of an eye? Do you realize what this will do to our family? Did you even think about that before you opened your mouth?"

I swallow and lift my chin. I refuse to let her ruin this moment for me. "You weren't protecting me when you told me to stay quiet," I say. "You were protecting yourself. I realize this will be tough for all of us, but if you really love me, you'll at least try to understand where I'm coming from and why I need to do this."

My mother leans over and rests her head against my father's arm.

He reaches out and touches my hand. In his eyes, I see him struggling to make sense of this. I squeeze his hand, then release it. He turns his attention back to Mom, guiding her inside the courthouse where it's cool and quiet.

I turn and gaze out into the crowd. Police officers are keeping the reporters off the steps near me, but I spot Knox standing just a few feet away, motioning to one of the officers.

I smile and walk up to them. "It's okay," I say. "He's with me."

The officer turns and nods, lifting his arm to let Knox through. I smile as I notice he's dressed in a suit and tie. The jacket is slung across his shoulder in the Georgia heat.

He approaches me with tears in his eyes. I throw my arms

SARRA CANNON

around him and pull him behind the pillar at the edge of the walkway. His coat falls to the ground at our feet.

He tenses and looks around to see if anyone is watching us. "I don't want to make this harder for you," he says. "I just wanted to tell you how much I love you and how very proud I am."

I smile and wipe a tear from his cheek. "I love you, too," I say. "And I want to do this the right way. No lies. No hiding. Just the truth."

Then, without a care in the world about who sees us together, I grab his tie and pull him in for a kiss.

CHAPTER 50

My legs burn with the fatigue of all the trips up and down three flights of stairs to my new apartment.

I was able to get a place one building over from Jenna's apartment, and I feel such a rush of overwhelming pride as I turn the key in the lock and push open the door.

My own place.

It feels so different from that first day in the dorms up in Boston. There, I was still being watched by a Resident Assistant. I was still following the university's rules. I was still forbidden from having boys in my room.

I was still in this in-between point where I had some level of independence, but my life wasn't really my own.

I look at my new apartment and smile. This place is all mine for the next twelve months. I can paint the walls, hang pictures, cook.

Or not. I can eat greasy take-out every night instead.

I can invite anyone I want and stay up as late as I want.

For now, the place is practically empty. The sum total of my belongings comes to three suitcases and six half-packed boxes. No couch. No pots and pans. Hell, I don't even have a bed yet.

It took most of the money I'd saved to be able to afford the deposit and first month's rent at this place.

Knox offered to help me pay, but what kind of independence would that be? No, I want to do this on my own.

As much as I love Knox, I want to claim this space for myself. I want to create my own tranquil space where I can just sit and think about what it is that I expect of myself. What do I really want out of my life? What do I want to be? What do I want to accomplish?

My whole life, people have saddled me with their expectations. Their rules. My parents, my teachers, my boyfriends, my schools. Even my best friends all expected something specific from me at some time or another. And I let them. I let their fear and their needs be my compass, always guiding my path.

But not anymore.

This place is mine.

And I just threw away my compass. It's time for a fresh start. It's time to figure out who Leigh Anne Davis really is deep down inside.

I close the apartment door, throw the deadbolt and walk into the center of the room where the boxes are piled up.

I sit down next to the first box, slit it open.

And begin to unpack.

CHAPTER 51

Jenna squeals as she pushes off from the shore and flies over the water, finally letting go and plunging into the water where Colton is waiting for her.

I laugh and pop another strawberry into my mouth.

Knox nods toward the bowl of fruit. I pick one up and move close to him, lifting the berry to his lips. He opens his mouth and takes a bite, the juice dripping down his chin. I smile as he wipes away the juice, then I lean forward and kiss him.

"Jesus, get a room," Penny says.

We pull away and she winks at me. She's been more supportive and understanding in all this than I gave her credit for. She's upset I didn't confide in her sooner, but she understands why and has been here for me along the way as a shoulder to lean on.

Her gaze moves from us to something in the distance. Sadness crosses her expression and I turn to see Mason and Preston walking up. Mason has his arm around some girl I've never seen before. As usual. I reach out and touch Penny's hand and she rolls her eyes, but I can see she's fighting back tears.

"He's an idiot," I say.

"Yes, he is," she says. "But so am I."

Joey sets a steaming plate of roasted corn on the cob in the center of the table and my mouth waters. "Where is everyone else?" she asks. "The food's almost ready."

I point toward the lake where Jenna is getting ready for yet another ride on the rope. Colton runs up behind her and lifts her high into the air. He gets a running start and jumps into the water, pulling her under. Krystal and Summer sit at the edge of the dock with their feet dangling in the water, watching.

"Can you call them up?" she asks me. "Knox, will you help me grab the rest of the food from the kitchen?"

"Sure," he says. He leans down and kisses me again and pure happiness rushes through me. He holds on to my hand as long as he can before the distance breaks us apart.

I watch him disappear into the house, unable to take my eyes off of him. I still can't believe he's mine. The media coverage has been just as brutal as we expected, but we're managing it fine. We spend most of our time out here at the lake when we can. The press can't come on private property, so we're sheltered out here to some degree. My parents are still freaking out from time to time, but are making an effort to get to know Knox, which makes me happy.

I still haven't told them the news Knox hit me with shortly after the press conference. It turns out he and his half-sisters equally inherited their father's fortune and Knox has over ten million dollars sitting in a bank account in Chicago.

I decided to let them suffer for a little while longer, though. I want them to learn to love and appreciate him for who he really is. Not to suddenly approve of him because of his money.

I finally look away and see that Penny is smiling at me, a twinkle in her eyes.

"What?" A blush creeps up my neck and my cheeks flush red.

She shakes her head. "As much as I would have loved to have had you for a sister-in-law, I have to say I've never seen you so happy."

I stand and take her arm in mine. We walk together toward the dock to call the others up to dinner. "I'm glad you're here," I say.

A lump forms in my throat and I pull a deep breath in through my nose, determined not to get too emotional. My friends have all really rallied around me lately. It feels amazing to know I have so much support, especially after a year and a half of my mother insisting the truth would ruin my life.

Instead, the truth has given me a freedom I never dreamed of. Here, in the presence of my closest friends, I don't have to hide anything. I don't have to lie or be fake or pretend I'm not hurting. I just have to be myself, and it's the best feeling in the world.

After dinner's over and everyone else has left for home, Knox and I sit on the porch drinking a glass of Joey's home-made wine.

"Thank you for today," I say. "I really needed that."

Knox smiles. "What's a lake house for if not for hanging out with friends and having good times?"

I look up at the beautiful house. It's still a work in progress, but Knox stayed true to his promise of getting it livable by the end of the summer. He officially moved in two weeks ago, and although I have my own apartment near Jenna's, I plan to spend a lot of time out here when I get home from Boston.

"Are you nervous about tomorrow?" he asks.

Nervous doesn't even begin to describe what I'm feeling.

Our flight to Boston leaves at noon. Sophy has agreed to meet us at the airport, and I'm looking forward to seeing her. I want to make sure she knows I don't blame her for what happened.

I am scheduled to meet with the attorney later that afternoon. Shortly after the press conference, Molly's attorney called me to say that several other girls had seen me on TV and been inspired to come forward. It broke my heart to know Burke had truly hurt so many women. The plan is to get everyone together tomorrow and see who is interested in moving forward with a trial.

"I hope the others come too," I say. I know from experience that it's not easy to tell the truth. Not everyone can, and that's okay. We all have to do what's right for our own lives and our own situations. Still, I can't help thinking that if I had had the courage to speak up sooner, I could have put Burke Redfield in jail a long time ago.

My life is a daily struggle to balance guilt, fear, and courage. Like the lake house, I'm still a work in progress.

Knox slips his hand around my waist and pulls me onto his lap. I smile and wrap my arms around his neck.

"Are you finished packing?" he asks. "Or do you need to get back to your place to finish up?"

I press my lips to his forehead, then his temple.

"I packed before I came over this afternoon," I say. "Why?"

His blue eyes sparkle when he looks at me and it sends a flutter through my chest. "Because right now, there is nothing I want to do in this world more than carry you up those stairs and make love to you until the sun comes up."

And that's exactly what he does.

CHAPTER 52

I have a death-grip on Knox's hand as we stand outside the attorney's office.

"What if I'm the only one?" I whisper.

Even my knees are trembling, and I curse the decision to wear high heels instead of something sensible and tremble-proof. I'm afraid that if I take a step forward, my knees might just give out and send me crashing to the floor.

Knox looks deep into my eyes. "You just tell your truth. Your experience," he says. "There's more power in that than you realize, Leigh Anne. You are strong. You can do this."

He places his hand on my face and caresses my cheek with his thumb.

"Thank you for being here," I say.

"I'm going to be here with you every step of the way, I promise," he says. His lips descend on mine and I lean in, pressing close to him.

I take a deep breath in and out. I lift my head up high.

I nod and Knox steps forward and grabs the large silver handle on the conference room door.

My breath quickens as the door opens. I slowly, carefully place one foot in front of the other and step into the room.

My heart skips a beat as four pairs of eyes turn toward me.

Eyes like mine.

Haunted. But full of hope.

THE MOMENT WE BEGAN

The moment they believe all hope is lost is the moment something real finally begins.

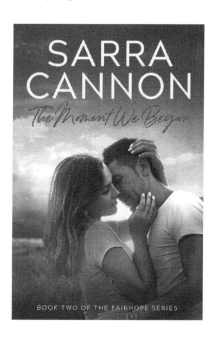

THE MOMENT WE BEGAN

Read Penny & Mason's Story

I hope you loved The Trouble With Goodbye. Writing book was such a healing experience for me, as many of Leigh Anne's experiences came from some of my own.

If you want to see how things progress with Leigh Anne's trial and to see how each of her best friends grow and fall in love, buy book 2, The Moment We Began now.

This second book is Penny and Mason's story, and it starts off a bit more rough and tumble, but at its core, it's a heart-warming and beautiful story just like this one.

Read The Moment We Began now.

Or, if you know you already love this town and Leigh Anne & her friends, you can get almost $9 OFF the entire series price when you buy The Complete Fairhope Series Bundle.

Buy the Bundle Here.

I genuinely hope you love spending time in Fairhope.

If you have a moment, I'd love for you to leave a review for The Trouble With Goodbye. Thank you with all my heart.

Sarra

❧

Love Sarra's books? Join Sarra's Mailing List to join the fan family and get book updates and more!

ABOUT THE AUTHOR

Sarra Cannon is the author of several series featuring young adult and college-aged characters, including the bestselling Shadow Demons Saga. Her novels often stem from her own experiences growing up in the small town of Hawkinsville, Georgia, where she learned that being popular always comes at a price and relationships are rarely as simple as they seem.

Sarra owns her own publishing company and has sold three-quarters of a million copies of her books. She currently lives in

Charleston, South Carolina with her programmer husband, her adorable redheaded son, and her beautiful daughter.

Love Sarra's books? Join Sarra's Mailing List to be notified of new releases and giveaways!

Also, please come hang out with me in my Facebook Fan Group: Sarra Cannon's Coven. We have a lot of fun in there, and I often share exclusive short stories and teasers in the group.

Want more? Come join us LIVE several times a week on my YouTube channel.

Connect With Sarra Online:
www.sarracannon.com

Made in the USA
Middletown, DE
11 June 2024

55602280R00137